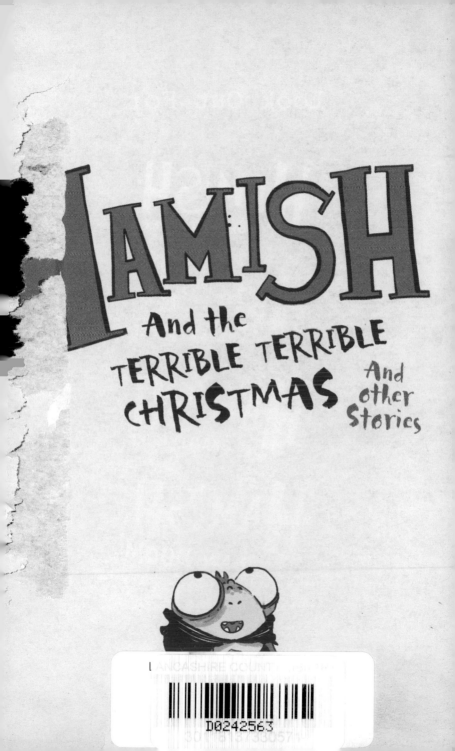

HAMISH

And the
TERRIBLE TERRIBLE
CHRISTMAS And other Stories

LANCASHIRE COUNT

D0242563

Look Out For

HAMISH
AND THE
WORLDSTOPPERS

HAMISH
AND THE
NEVERPEOPLE

HAMISH
AND THE
GRAVITYBURP

HAMISH
AND THE
BABY BOOM!

HAMISH

And the
TERRIBLE TERRIBLE
CHRISTMAS And other Stories

DANNY WALLACE

ILLUSTRATED
BY
JAMIE
LITTLER

SIMON & SCHUSTER

LONDON   NEW YORK   SYDNEY   TORONTO   NEW DELHI   STARKLEY

Lancashire Library Services	
30118137330571	
PETERS	JF
£6.99	15-Feb-2019
NST	

First published in Great Britain in 2018 by Simon and Schuster UK Ltd

A CBS COMPANY
Text Copyright © Danny Wallace 2018

Illustrations Copyright © Jamie Littler 2018
This book is copyright under the Berne Convention.
No reproduction without permission. All rights reserved.

The right of Danny Wallace and Jamie Littler to be identified as the author
and illustrator of this work has been asserted by them in accordance with
sections 77 and 78 of the Copyright, Design and Patent Act, 1988.

1 3 5 7 9 10 8 6 4 2

Simon & Schuster UK Ltd
1st Floor, 222 Gray's Inn Road
London
WC1X 8HB

www.simonandschuster.co.uk

Simon & Schuster Australia, Sydney
Simon & Schuster India, New Delhi

A CIP catalogue record for this book is available from the British Library.

PB ISBN 978-1-4711-7657-9
eBook ISBN 978-1-4711-7656-2

This book is a work of fiction. Names, characters, places and
incidents are either the product of the author's imagination
or are used fictitiously. Any resemblance to actual people
living or dead, events or locales is entirely coincidental.

Printed and bound by CPI Group (UK) Ltd, Croydon, CR0 4YY
Simon & Schuster UK Ltd are committed to sourcing paper that is made
from wood grown in sustainable forests and supports the Forest Stewardship
Council, the leading international forest certification organisation. Our
books displaying the FSC logo are printed on FSC certified paper.

CONTENTS

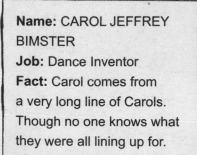

Madame Cous Cous presents

Christmas Carols

Name: CAROL JEFFREY BIMSTER
Job: Dance Inventor
Fact: Carol comes from a very long line of Carols. Though no one knows what they were all lining up for.

Name: CAROL BARRELL
Job: Local Explorer
Fact: Carol has trouble pronouncing words that begin with an F or a TH. So she can't say fairer than that.

Venk's Christmas Cracker Joke

Q. *What do you call a very terrible Terrible?*

A. *A Verri-ble!*

Name: CAROLE TOPP-SOIL
Job: Bank Manager
Fact: Carole added an "E" to her name so she wouldn't be chosen for this display as she has a full-time job, but that didn't worke.

NORWEGIANS ALWAYS WELCOME

Kids Eat Free on Christmas Day!

Alice's Christmas Cracker Joke

Q. *What do you call a really boring villain?*

A. *Axel blah-blah-BLAH-marsh!*

STARKLEY FM

It's not boring!

FM Schedule

6 a.m.

The Sound of Starkley

The only breakfast show to bring you the true sound of Starkley at Christmas, from a microphone we hang out of our window. Hear the sound of a passing bus at Christmas! Or a distant conversation about eggs! It's not boring.

10 a.m.

Janice Mad

To celebrate Christmas, on today's show Janice will talk about the history of benches. It's not boring. Plus *"Janice Mad's Big Bad Name Game'*. Can Janice guess your name just from the sound of you saying it out loud? She has never got it right before!

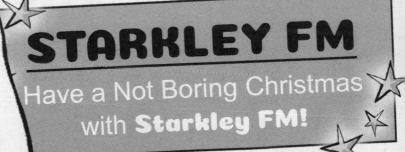

STARKLEY FM

Have a Not Boring Christmas with *Starkley FM!*

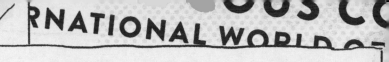

1 p.m.

Tony Graze

What's this week's mystery sound? (It's a car alarm) Tony also tries to guess the tunes of Christmas songs he's found written down on the internet. Plus the brand new game Map or Nap? Is the silence you hear for thirty minutes the sound of a map? Or has Tony left the studio to have a nap? Note: no prizes.

3 p.m.

The Mayor's Christmas Address

After last year's controversy, this year the mayor will make sure he gets all his facts straight!

3.05 p.m.

The Mayor's Corrections

The Mayor of Starkley tells us what he got wrong in his speech.

3.10 p.m.

The Mayor's Clarifications

The Mayor of Starkley clarifies exactly what he meant in his corrections and apologises for any offence.

3.15 p.m.

The Mayor Responds to Complaints

The Mayor of Starkley offers his immediate resignation.

3.20 p.m.

Christmas Tuba Music

It's not boring.

HAMISH AND THE TERRIBLE TERRIBLE CHRISTMAS

Merry Christmas, Hamish!

Hamish Ellerby lay in bed and squeezed his eyes shut.

If there was one thing he knew for certain, it was that he was about to have the best sleep *ever.*

Lots of kids can't sleep on Christmas Eve. They're too busy thinking about Santa and presents and whether their Uncle Jeremy will eat all the Brussels sprouts and stink out the front room again.

But Hamish never had any trouble sleeping. He just wanted the night out of the way. It was very late and tomorrow would be a big day.

Everyone would be up at six a.m., for a start.

In the Ellerby household, Hamish and his older brother Jimmy would fling themselves out of bed and rush to the tree in the living room.

They'd sit and wait and stare at the presents.

And then they'd sit and wait and stare some more.

At five past six, Jimmy would quietly feel the wrapping and make wild guesses about what they might contain.

"I think Mum's got me a piranha!" he'd say, holding up what was quite obviously a book. "Or maybe it's a motorbike!"

Then the two boys would sit and wait and stare some more.

At about quarter to eight, Dad would *finally* get up and have a really long wee which the whole house would hear. Sometimes these wees were so long that Hamish thought his dad must be just standing there, drinking a never-ending bottle of water, constantly refilling himself. Meanwhile the boys would be inching closer to the presents, ready for . . .

PHEEEEEEEEP!

Mum would blow her Special Christmas Whistle, and Hamish and Jimmy would dive forward, tearing their presents open and making wild whooping sounds, even if all that was inside was just a packet of nuts or a thimble.

Then Dad would drive to the 24-hour garage to buy batteries for all the things he'd forgotten to buy batteries for and pick up some Chocolate Mustn'tgrumbles or a newspaper to give to Mum as an extra present, while she made her special Christmas fry-up.

After that it would be playing and cartoons, a visit to Madame Cous Cous's International World of Treats, and then, just before lunchtime, all the residents of the town would head to the school hall to sing songs and wish everyone a happy Christmas. That was a nice bit. They'd all sing the official Starkley Christmas Song, written by Hamish's teacher, Mr Longblather. It didn't rhyme very well or make much sense, because Mr Longblather was better at teaching geography than music. It went:

OH, STARKLEY IS A
LOVELY LITTLE TOWN,
ONE WHERE WE SMILE AND
WE NEVER REALLY FROWN,
BUT THAT'S NOT ENTIRELY TRUE,
BECAUSE SOMETIMES
WE FROWN,
BUT THE POINT IS THAT
IT'S CHRISTMAS!

Doesn't sound too bad, does it?

Except that it goes on.

And on.

It goes on for about fifteen minutes!

Just the same words over and over!

Then, *at last* – it would be off to crowd around the town clock. The clock was the symbol of Starkley. Starkley just wouldn't be Starkley without it. Everyone would pretend to listen to the mayor making a speech, and then he'd switch on all the brightly-coloured lights all around it, and everyone would clap and eat biscuits and go home for a big Christmas dinner.

It was going to be GREAT! So Hamish knew it was vital he fell asleep as quickly as possible, to get the boring night bit out of the way.

But just as his eyes had gone droopy, and his arms limp, and his pillow was starting to go soggy from all his drool . . .

"Hamish!" came a voice in an urgent half-whisper. "*HAMISH!*"

Up and At 'Em!

Hamish did one of those weird jolty sleep jumps you sometimes make.

His eyes shot open.

"Hamish, *wake up*," said the voice, now a little louder.

"Dad?" said Hamish.

He flicked his bedside light on and aimed it at the door, to see his father, Angus Ellerby, dressed all in black and with his hands on his hips.

On Dad's top was a small image of a sunflower with two wings; the official logo of **Belasko**. The company his dad pretended just made boring things like matches and tiles and paper – but which was actually in charge of protecting the world from its enemies.

"Put your suit on," said Dad. "There's trouble."

Now, those of you who have read about Hamish before will know all about Belasko and Hamish's dad's involvement. You'll know that they've fought off Terribles together and saved Starkley many times before. But at the time this story is set, his dad's secret life is all very new to Hamish.

Because this was all happening the very same Christmas Hamish's dad disappeared, so before the events of *Hamish and the Worldstoppers* even happened. Before Hamish even knew any of the **PDF** and they started taking on evil themselves.

But hang on, I can hear you thinking. *Hamish didn't know his dad was some kind of super-agent back then, did he?*

Well, I really think you need to start trusting people more. You seem to have serious issues in that department. Just go with it, because everything will become clear very soon . . .

Hamish met his dad at the foot of the stairs, lit by the glow of the Christmas lights from the living room.

They were wearing matching outfits now. Black trousers, a black top, black cap, black army boots and, of course, the Belasko patch.

"What do you *mean* there's trouble?" asked Hamish, snapping on his gloves.

Hamish had known his dad was a Belasko agent for some

time now, ever since the night of his tenth birthday, when he couldn't sleep and had heard his dad talking on the phone to someone called Alex.

He'd used words like **"invasion"**, **"monsters"**, **"evil"** and **"aliens"**. It was very hard for Dad to pretend it was a normal work call with an assistant regional manager after that!

It was super-important to keep all this a secret from Mum. She was such a worrier. She wouldn't even have let Hamish have a stick insect, because she thought he might poke himself in the eye with it. And even though Hamish and his brother talked about *everything*, he couldn't tell Jimmy, because Jimmy was on Twitter and there is nothing a fourteen-year-old won't tell people on Twitter.

So it was Hamish and Dad's secret.

@jimmyellerby ✈ FOLLOW
I AM EATING SOUP

↩ ⟲ 0 ★ 0

@jimmyellerby ✈ FOLLOW
I AM LOOKING AT A TREE

↩ ⟲ 0 ★ 0

@jimmyellerby 🐦 FOLLOW

I JUST PEED OUT THAT SOUP

↩ ⇄ 0   ★ 0

In return for keeping quiet, Dad had been giving him basic agent training. They'd pretend they were playing Boggle each night in Hamish's room, but as soon as the door was closed, his dad would tell him stories of aliens and monsters and of a race of super-intelligent beasts called the **Superiors**. He'd teach him combat moves he said might come in handy one day, like the Crab Kick or the Swiss Roll. And he'd give important nuggets of advice, like "You must always be prepared, Hamish! Always!"

But Hamish had never been part of an actual real-life mission before.

"Come on," said his dad. "To the car!"

3

The Cliffs

The Vectra seemed to purr as they motored through Starkley.

Everything was dark and twinkly and lit by the orange blush of the streetlights. The town's big Christmas tree, with its baubles and tinsel, looked beautiful. The nativity scene was in place. There were decorations in every window, and the town clock told them it was nearly midnight. It seemed like everybody was tucked up in bed except Hamish and his dad.

"Look!" said Hamish, pointing up at the sky. "It's starting to snow!"

All the kids of Starkley wanted was a white Christmas. Everyone wanted Christmas to be like it is on TV, instead of the usual grey and wind and drizzle. Well, not this year! They could get their sleds out! It was going to be ace!

"Focus, Hamish," said his dad as they raced down

Flycatcher Lane. They were headed for the old grey bridge. That meant that soon they'd be at the cliffs.

"Where are we going, Dad?" asked Hamish, worried.

Kids weren't really allowed over the old grey bridge, much. His dad certainly warned him off it.

"It seems there's a plan afoot," said his dad. "A plan to rob Starkley of its morale."

Hamish didn't really know what that meant, so didn't say anything, because he didn't want to seem like he wasn't a real agent. But it sounded bad.

Over the bridge they drove, and soon they were motoring down a small road, surrounded by dark swaying trees. It was stormier here and the rising roar of the nearby sea gave Hamish goosepimples. The snow was growing heavier, but without all the lights and general feeling of goodwill, it didn't feel like Christmas had reached this bit of town at all. But Hamish was with his dad, and his dad made him feel brave. Plus he was in uniform, and costumes do wonders for bravery. That's why right now I'm dressed as a cowboy.

Dad slowed the car to a halt.

"I brought you here because it's important you know what we're up against," he said. "I want you to see it first-hand. In case you ever need to act."

Hamish nodded, but again didn't really know what his dad meant. Act? He rarely needed to act. He'd been cast as a mouse in the last school play and didn't even have any lines. He just had to squeak and then walk off.

Dad opened the car door and Hamish followed suit. They padded through some undergrowth and into some bushes and before they knew it they were right at the edge of the cliffs.

"Look!" said his dad, over the crash of the waves.

Down there, in the violent sea, was a huge black shape.

As Hamish's eyes adjusted, he realized it was a ship. But not a ferry, or a galleon . . . it was some kind of enormous grey battleship!

On the side, in shaky white letters, was scrawled . . .

HMS CARRAS

"What does HMS mean?" asked Hamish.

"It stands for Her Majesty's Ship," said his dad. "But this does not look like one of the Queen's."

It certainly didn't. And it seemed very unlikely she was on board. It was Christmas Eve. She was probably trying to guess what her presents were or watching telly.

And this ship was fearsome. It was long and sharp and as grey as a shark. Huge waves battered against it, but it held still and firm.

Hamish heard the distant eery clanking of a bell and then . . .

"What on EARTH is THAT?" said Hamish, suddenly absolutely terrified.

4

BUUUUUH!

On the deck of the ship, a large black shadow had appeared. It looked ginormous. No, forget that. It looked super-*ginor*-massive!

But it soon became clear it wasn't **one** thing – it was **many**.

A dozen thrunkling, hurkling shapes huffered about, shifting crates. Hamish's dad crouched and sighed.

"Terribles," he said gravely.

"What?!" asked Hamish, who'd never seen such things before. "Why are they called Terribles?"

"Well . . ." said his dad, wondering how to put this. "It's mainly because they're terrible."

Which was obvious now he'd said it.

"Terribles are sent to do whatever terrible things their masters want," Dad continued, handing Hamish some binoculars. "Here. What else can you see?"

Hamish pressed them to his eyes and immediately put

them down again.

Terribles were *disgusting!* Slithery, scaly, spitty, clawy and *gross*. Bigger than Dad, with mean eyes and beige teeth.

Bravely, Hamish took another look. What he saw confused him.

"They're carrying enormous heaters!" he said. "And some kind of windmill! And they've got strange stripy hooks. And I can see a box marked **EXPLOSIVES!** And one of them is holding a picture of something . . ."

"What is it, Hamish?" said his dad, as the wind rose and snowflakes danced around them. "Look harder."

Hamish frowned.

"It's a picture of the *town clock!*"

The air filled with the sound of a low, loud horn from the ship.

BUUUUUUUU UUUUUUUUUH.

The trees around Hamish shook and vibrated. A huge dollop of snow dropped from a branch and landed on his head. And then another. But Hamish didn't care. For far down below, three small boats dropped from the side of HMS CARRAS and crashed into the choppy waters. Slimy, sickly, slavering Terribles hurled themselves into them and began to row to shore.

"What are they planning?" asked Hamish nervously. "Why are they here?"

"They're here," said his dad importantly, "to *ruin Christmas*."

5

Land Ahoy!

"Here's what we know," said Dad, reversing the Vectra and spinning it round. "They're working on a plan to turn the people of Starkley against each other. I'm not sure how, yet. But this must be the first stage. They want to ruin Christmas so that we don't have any good memories of it and to start turning us against each other."

Hamish thought about it as his dad drove. What did all this have to do with the town clock? Maybe the Terribles were going to blow it up with those explosives.

That seemed a little unnecessary, if you asked Hamish. A little *dramatic*. Maybe they should just give the clock to the Terribles. It always seemed to run a bit fast these days, anyway.

"We're going to have to follow the Terribles," said his dad. "It could be dangerous. Do you want to go home?"

Hamish did. He wanted to go home like nothing else. He wanted to climb back into his bed, pull his covers over his eyes and just hope Christmas went back to normal. But he couldn't leave his dad to do this on his own. And what if he woke up and Christmas was never normal again? He would feel so guilty that he didn't do more.

"I'm coming with you," he said. "I'm a junior Belasko agent."

"Good lad," said his dad.

And he flipped down his sun shield and pressed a button Hamish had never seen before, marked **TURBO**. They **BOOMED** over the bridge.

Down at the shore, minutes later, Hamish and his dad hid in some bushes as the first of the Terribles' rickety little boats made it to land.

"Put this on," instructed his dad, handing Hamish a balaclava. "If they spot us, I don't want them *ever* to recognize you."

Hamish pulled it over his face.

The second and third boats arrived, and the twelve Terribles HEEEEAVED their equipment out.

The ground was white with snow now. On reflection, Hamish decided they probably shouldn't have dressed entirely in black. Maybe dressing in white would have been better.

The beasts split up and moved slowly towards the town.

"We'll follow that group," said his dad, pointing at the most terrifying Terribles of all, and together the two Ellerbys stayed low and crept after them from a distance. They were heading into the forest. Hamish wanted to reach out for his dad's hand. But he had to be brave.

"It's okay, H," said Dad. "Take my hand."

The monsters' giant heaters and tall windmills and boxes and hooks teetered perilously on their backs as they grunted and growled and left huge, heavy footprints in the snow.

After what seemed an age, one Terrible checked his map and signalled to the others. The snow was getting really heavy now, and the beasts were struggling. One of them got the giant heater out while his friends pushed the tall windmill to its feet.

CLANK

It was up.

What were they doing?

BRAAAW–RAW–RAWWL

A Terrible pulled at a cord to start the heater's engine.

It wiped the snow from its eyes and tried again.

BRAAAAAWVVVVVV

The heater's metal grille glowed orange. Hamish felt the heat immediately.

Now the windmill had started. Slowly, the giant blades began to turn.

WOOOOV
WOOOOV
WOOOOV

"What's happening?" asked Hamish, as wave after wave of heat hit him and the trees began to sway from the sheer power of the wind.

Around them, the snowflakes began to shoot and shimmy madly in the air. Hamish realized that his face was now completely wet. His balaclava was stuck to his face. His legs were really heavy. He was soaked.

"They're melting the snow," said his dad. "They're destroying our white Christmas! And then they're going to **steal our clock!**"

6

Silent Night

As Hamish and his dad clambered back into the car the three giant windmills that now surrounded Starkley were blowing the heat right across town, so that while the rest of the country was getting a blizzard, in Starkley there was an absolute downpour as the snow in the air melted into rain.

"What do they want with our clock?" asked Hamish, shivering from the cold water as the rain battered the windshield.

"I only know one thing," said his dad, starting the car. "HMS CARRAS is an anagram. I didn't realize at first. But now I see that if you rearrange the letters . . . it spells SCARMARSH."

Hamish frowned. What did that mean?

"Scarmarsh is pure evil. He is working on a way to stop time itself."

"Stop *time?*"

That seemed insane! Who'd believe *that?*

"He must think there's something special about the town clock."

As they got closer to town, Hamish suddenly had a thought.

"Dad . . . what if they're at home when we get there? What if there's . . . a Terrible in my room?"

His dad smiled gently.

"They hate water. There's no way they'll come to Starkley while all this rain is coming. They'll stand behind the heaters, where it's still snowing. For now, we go home and pretend like nothing's happened."

Hamish felt a little better. Until his dad turned to him, and said, very seriously . . .

"It's when the rain *stops* that we have to worry."

WH

Hamish didn't sleep at all well that night. The sound of the rain falling heavily over Starkley was both a comfort and a concern.

Sometime around six a.m., he felt an arm on his shoulder and jolted from his sleep.

A Terrible! A TERRIBLE!

AAAAAARRRRGH!

Hamish grabbed the small foam baseball bat he'd put next to his bed and swung it wildly around.

YES! A direct HIT!

"OW!" shouted Jimmy, clutching his head. **"WHAT DID YOU DO THAT FOR?"**

Whoops.

"Happy Christmas, Jimmy," said Hamish, pretending he'd just acted in a completely normal way. "Just thought I'd bop you on the head."

"You blinkin' NOODLEBEAR!" shouted his brother. **"I was only blinkin' WAKING YOU UP!"**

And then Hamish realized something with horror.

Apart from Jimmy going "ow" and hopping around and then saying words he really should *not* be saying, Starkley was silent.

Heart-stoppingly, brain-bruisingly *silent*.

The rain had stopped.

Morning is Broken

For the first year since Hamish could remember, no one had to wait for Dad to get up at quarter to eight and have a pee so long you might as well call it a peeeeeeeeeeeeeeeeee.

He was already in the living room, sitting on an armchair, facing the door.

He winked at Hamish as he walked in. He'd been sitting up all night, just in case.

He probably **really** needed the bog.

Hamish glanced out of the window. The weather was as dull as could be. There was no snow, there was no rain. The heaters in the forests around town were drying the clouds and chasing the puddles away.

It was just another grey, grey, boring Christmas Day in Starkley.

From upstairs, Mum blew her whistle.

"PRESENTS!" shouted Jimmy, throwing himself

into the pile and starting to rip.

Hamish stood closer to his dad.

"I've worked it out," said his dad quietly. "Just before lunch. That's when every resident of Starkley will be in the school hall singing the Starkley song. The Terribles won't want to be seen. So that must be when they'll steal the clock."

Hamish took a deep breath and nodded. He felt a little more relaxed now that he knew a Terrible wasn't about to burst through the door.

"Now go and open some presents and act like a kid," said his dad, smiling, and Hamish suddenly felt the excitement that every kid should feel on Christmas Day.

He dived in after Jimmy and started to rip the presents open.

"Happy Christmas, nitwits!" said his mum, carrying in two cups of tea and some **MUSTN'TGRUMBLES** on a tray filled with holly. "Hamish, did we ever tell you that if you'd been born a girl, we would have called you Holly?"

Jimmy rolled his eyes and smiled at his brother. Their mum said that *every* year.

For the rest of that Christmas morning, while Mum got ready, Hamish and Jimmy just carried on like everything was normal. They read their new Captain

Beetlebottom annuals and gorged on Chomps. Hamish was always gorging on Chomps. So much so that even though he brushed his teeth every morning and night, Dad had booked him an appointment at The Tooth Hurts. It wasn't for months, but he'd said: "Prevention's as good as the cure, Hamish! Always be prepared!"

Despite all the chocolate, Hamish couldn't enjoy the morning. He kept one eye on the clock.

"Right!" said his mum, wearing her best coat. "It's time! Let's make this a Christmas to remember!"

Hamish looked at his dad.

Oh, it would be *that*, all right.

Snow Joke

Hamish opened the front door of his house and cast a beady eye around.

He looked at the bushes. And at the bins. And at the end of the garden.

There were no Terribles to be seen.

"Come on, then, let's start walking!" said his mum, and the little family walked from their house on Lovelock Close, past the post office, to the town square. They passed Mr Slackjaw, who was outside Slackjaw's Motors using the unusually warm weather to wash all his shiny mopeds with his enormous red hosepipe.

People were already milling excitedly around near the town's big Christmas tree. Some of the kids were staring up at the sky, sadly holding new sleds they'd hoped to use.

Buster, who Hamish had seen around school, zoomed past on a new scooter. He'd only had it two hours but he'd already added the engine from an old lawnmower to the back and now it did nearly forty miles an hour. A kid called Elliot must have been given a new science set, because he was wandering around wearing goggles, poking things with a long metal prodder.

Hamish's friend Robin had a new football, because he always managed to lose his somehow. Just inside Lord of the Fries, some fierce-looking girl with a golden stripe through her hair was spending her Christmas money on fishburgers. And everyone seemed to be carrying a brand new Christmas sweet from lovely old **Madame Cous Cous**, who let everybody eat for free on Christmas Day.

"So far so normal," said Hamish.

"Right," said his mum, sighing. "Let's go and sing this extremely long song."

But as they joined the mass of people all heading to the Winterbourne School Hall, Hamish's dad placed his hand on Hamish's shoulder.

"Oh, no!" he said.

Hamish immediately froze.

"What is it?" said his mum.

"I forgot to buy batteries!" replied Dad. "Hamish, will you come with me? I don't want to go to a garage on my own on Christmas Day again!"

"But you'll miss the extremely long song!" said Mum sadly. "The one that's just the same over and over and over again!"

Hamish's dad smiled cheekily. That didn't sound so bad when she said it out loud, did it?

"Go on, then!" she said. "Me and Jimmy will just sing twice as loud!"

Jimmy was furious. How come **Hamish** got to go to a 24-hour garage to buy batteries on Christmas Day and *he* didn't?

Actually, he thought, *that sounds even worse*.

Hamish and his dad waited until they were out of sight, and then waited a little longer until every other resident of Starkley – from Frau Fussbundler to horrible school bully Grenville Bile to rat-nosed Scratch Tuft and rat-eared Mole Stunk – had followed them in.

As he passed, Grenville made a face at Hamish, and grunted, "Merry Christmas, **Smell**erby."

He *always* picked on Hamish.

"Don't worry about him," said his dad, as the doors of the school closed. "We've got some Terribles to stop!"

46

All Creatures
Great and
Terrible

Hamish and his dad hid round the back of the post office where they could keep a really good eye on the town clock.

They'd dashed back home really quickly to get their Belasko suits and now they looked the business. Hamish's dad had insisted Hamish put on his balaclava again too.

From a distance, they could hear the sounds of Madame Cous Cous playing the organ drift over town. That meant the Terribles could too. Any second now...

♪ OH, STARKLEY IS A
LOVELY LITTLE TOWN,
ONE WHERE WE SMILE AND
WE NEVER REALLY FROWN...

"Dad," said Hamish. "Even though we're probably about to come face to face with a horde of marauding monsters who want to destroy our entire way of life, I'm still really pleased I'm not in that hall singing that song."

His dad laughed.

And he was about to reply, when the noise began.

A skittery, skattery noise. A hum that rose in volume and intensity. A smell that seemed to come from nowhere. The smell of old eggs and damp carpet and dogs' bottoms.

They still couldn't see any Terribles.

Suddenly, an old metal bin flew past the town clock, crashing into a wall and flinging old fish bones and stale coffee all over the pavement. Now the noise grew LOUDER, and Hamish could see them . . .

TERRIBLES.

Stalking into town, carrying their hooks, which they'd painted red and white to look like enormous Christmas candy canes!

They were wearing little elf hats and the most awful Christmas jumpers Hamish had ever seen. Jumpers that must have been knitted by someone's colour-blind aunt. A colour-blind aunt who couldn't actually knit and had also lost the use of her fingers.

One of the Terribles dropped the wooden crate Hamish had seen marked **EXPLOSIVES**. It used its hook to prise the lid off, and brought out massive black Christmas crackers. But not *normal* Christmas crackers. These must be Christmas crackers that *really* explode!

Another Terrible scampered and clawed its way to the top of the town Christmas tree, replacing all the baubles with spiky black conkers. It knocked the star off the top and put a little silver Terrible that was spitting sharp silver stars in its place.

Two more Terribles clacked up the tree after the first one, tugging and ripping all the tinsel down and replacing it with nasty barbed wire.

Another one replaced all the mince pies in Madame Cous Cous's shop window with *mice* pies, then swapped all the gingerbread men for gingerbread *Terribles* – made with so much ginger they made your eyes go tiny, your nostrils flare and your ears make a PFFFFFF sound.

They all began to cackle and hoot. Oh, they were ruining Christmas, all right!

Now they opened a fresh crate. Inside was every tool you could ever imagine. Lump hammers, saws, the lot. They were going to knock the clock down and take it away on a trolley!

"What do we do?" said Hamish, as his dad's mind raced.

OH, STARKLEY IS A
LOVELY LITTLE TOWN,
ONE WHERE WE SMILE AND
WE NEVER REALLY FROWN . . .

The people of Starkley were already on their third verse. Or was it their fourth? That was the problem with this song, no one really knew when it was coming to an end. The only clue you had was. . .

WHEN EVERYONE SANG THE LAST LINE, SLOOOOOOWWWW-LYYYYY.

"Dad?" said Hamish.

"Maybe we should call for back-up," he said.

"There isn't time!" said Hamish. "Look!"

The Terribles had started bashing at the bottom of the town clock with their lump hammers. They were doing it in time with the song, so it sounded like a drum beat and no one would notice.

They were sweating now. Hamish watched a bead of sweat snake down a Terrible's back then fall to the ground, where it fizzed on the concrete.

"Wait!" said Hamish. "It's snowing everywhere in the

country except Starkley, right?"

"Yes," said his dad. "There's a dome of heat over town. The heaters are now so hot they're keeping *all* the weather out."

"So what happens if we turn the heaters off? Will it start snowing again?"

"Yes," said his dad. "It'll get much colder very quickly. But how does that help?"

"You said the Terribles hate water," said Hamish, thinking.

"But the water will turn to ice . . ." said his dad, and then he stopped in his tracks. "Hamish, I think you're *onto something!*"

Let's Go!

This had to work!

Hamish's dad raced as quickly as he could back to the Vectra, jumped in, flipped his sun visor down, and hit TURBO.

The Terribles saw the car bolt away but carried on, regardless. Time was of the essence, and what did one witness matter now?

THUMP! THUMP! THUMP!

went the lump hammers.

Dusts of cloud blew from the top of the old clock as they weakened it.

Hamish looked at his wrist. His dad had handed him his watch before he left.

"Take the Explorer," he'd said. "When the heaters are off, I'll send you a signal. You'll know what it is."

Hamish took a deep breath.

OH, STARKLEY IS A LOVELY LITTLE TOWN,

Hamish grew scared. There couldn't be much time left. He'd heard those words dozens of times now. He stared at his dad's watch.

And then something amazing happened. It glowed green. The hands of the watch began to spin crazily round. The signal! Hamish looked up at the sky. It was like it was turning from light blue to ice white. It hurt just to look at it, it was so bright.

Quickly, he dashed to Slackjaw's Motors and picked up the heavy old red hosepipe with the brass nozzle. Mr Slackjaw had bought it second-hand from Frinkley Fire Station. He dragged it as close to the Terribles as he could without being seen, and ran back to the tap. But when should he turn it on?

And then Hamish noticed one, single, solitary snowflake falling to earth.

It landed on the ground. It didn't melt.

Another came.

And another.

A Terrible looked up at the sky, confused. It barked something at the others, who stopped bashing at the clock, and stared upwards.

Now thousands of snowflakes began to fall. The air became chilled. Even under his balaclava, Hamish felt the ice-cold sting in his cheeks.

NOW, he thought, and tried to turn on the water. But the tap was stuck and he hadn't noticed how cold and useless his hands had become. Desperately, he blew on them, and wrenched at the tap, but still it wouldn't budge!

"**BUUUUUUUUUUUUULAA AAAASSSSSKOOOOOO!**" came a voice from somewhere behind him. He turned to see a Terrible across the street, pointing a weathered, bony finger at him. "**BUULLLLAAAASSSSKOOOO!**"

Hamish had been spotted! And they thought he was a

proper agent! Not a ten-year-old boy!

Quickly, he thought. ***One last go!***

And he kicked at the tap. It moved. Wait! He should try the Crab Kick his dad taught him!

YES!

The sheer power of water suddenly rushing through the pipe made it rise high in the air, like an angry snake. Water shot from it by the gallon. The Terribles backed away, shrieking and cowering and putting limp hands over dreadful faces. Hamish grabbed the hose and tried to control it. It was so powerful that all he could do was hold on.

But the Terribles were getting soaked!

They tried to run, but as they did so the cold set in. It was *very* cold now. Hamish realized that his dad hadn't just turned off the heaters – he'd put them in reverse! Starkley was becoming like the Arctic!

They should rename it the Starktic!

The twelve fleeing, panicked Terribles couldn't get away. They were slooooooooowing down as they ran, their bodies covered by a thin layer of creeping ice that now spread right across their skin, their scales, their nooks and their crannies until all they could do . . .

. . . was just stand there.

Hamish blinked.

He had *frozen the Terribles!*

Seconds later, the Vectra skidded to a halt, flinging fresh snow everywhere.

"You did it, Hamish!" said Dad.

Just as, across the whole town, the song reached its crescendo . . .

BUT THE POINT IIIIIS
THAAAAAT IIIIIIT'S. . .
CHRIIIIISTMAAAAAS!

11

Let It Snow

As the townsfolk of Starkley all walked back to the main square from the school hall, it was clear that something had changed.

"It's SNOWING!" yelled one of the kids.

"It's a white Christmas!" screamed Mr Longblather in joy, which was weird, because no one had ever seen Mr Longblather happy about anything.

Everybody cheered. Every rooftop and pavement was thick with snow. They'd get to use their new sleds after all!

But as the people of Starkley got closer to the square, Hamish held his breath.

Would they notice?

"Who on earth was in charge of the nativity scene this year?" asked Madame Cous Cous, tapping her stick on the ground.

Everyone stood around and stared at it. No one had paid it much attention before, but now that they did, it looked rather . . . odd.

"What's happened to the wise men?" asked Frau Fussbundler. "They don't exactly look very wise. They look like they've got constipation."

Hamish and his dad played it casual.

"I think it's just a very unusual take on a classic Christmas scene," said Hamish's dad. "I like it."

Twelve Terribles stood completely frozen, dressed up in whatever the two Ellerbys had managed to find from the charity shop at extremely short notice.

"There's Jesus," said Madame Cous Cous, walking down the line. "And there's Mary. And there's a Manchester United Player. And a Samurai. I understand all that, because it's very Christmassey. But why is there one just dressed as a kitten in a bowler hat? Why is there a wasp with a trombone?"

"Anyway," said Hamish's dad, doing his best to

BOOOOOOOOOOOOM!

What the—?

Everyone turned to see Grenville Bile, his hair standing completely on end, and with a totally blackened face. In his hands was a rather large and dangerous-looking Christmas cracker.

"I must have forgotten to replace that one," whispered Dad, looking not entirely guilty.

Hamish really loved his dad.

"Right," said the mayor, climbing onto a crate still marked **EXPLOSIVES**. "Before you all go sledging and throwing snowballs and having the best Christmas that Starkley has ever had, it is time for my speech. And settle down. Because it's an extra long and rather *explosive* one this year!"

A few people took a step back.

Hamish didn't. And he didn't care how long this speech was.

Because it was *Christmas*. And he'd helped his dad on a *real* mission!

Nothing could go wrong now.

And then Dad's phone rang.

On the screen was a name.

Alex.

The End of the Beginning

The next day, Boxing Day, after Hamish and his dad had called **Belasko**, and had a certain nativity scene quietly taken away in a lorry, Hamish was a little uneasy.

Sometimes you feel like that after such a lot of excitement has passed. But still. He'd noticed that his dad was quite quiet. Ever since the phone call yesterday, he'd been a bit distant. Like there was something on his mind.

He was probably just tired. And anyway, *Star Wars* would be on tonight, and Dad said he wanted to watch it with his boys, and eat food that was bad for them on purpose.

But still. It was weird.

"Do you want to play Boggle in your room?" he asked Hamish, as Jimmy napped on the sofa. Hamish's eyes lit up.

"Another adventure?" he said hopefully.

"No," said his dad. "I'd just really like to play Boggle with you."

On Hamish's bed, they got the game out and began to play. But still his dad was quiet. He fiddled with a bag at the foot of the bed.

"Is something the matter?" asked Hamish.

Angus Ellerby took a moment.

"Yes, pal," he said. "I'm afraid there is."

Hamish's tummy sank.

His dad undid the strap of his watch and took it off.

"I want you to have this," he said. "Look after it, and it will look after you. It's an extra special Christmas present for saving Starkley."

"Wow," said Hamish, but deep down he knew this wasn't the only thing Dad was going to tell him.

"I have to go away, Hamish," his dad said. "And I don't know when I'll be back."

Hamish looked up at him with his huge greeny-brown eyes. Yesterday he'd felt ten feet tall. Right now he felt tiny.

"What do you mean?"

"I can't risk them finding out you helped me," he said. "It's too dangerous for you, for Mum and for Jimmy. It's my fault. I should never have involved you."

"But I like being involved!" said Hamish. "Please, Dad, you don't have to go! And go where? When?"

"Tonight," said Dad. "I have to go tonight. Scarmarsh is planning something and I can't let him come back to Starkley. I have to take the fight to him. Stop him before he gets here again."

"But . . . but what if he catches you?" said Hamish, trying to come up with anything to make his dad say this was all just a joke. "What if he gets you?"

"Promise me, Hamish. Promise me you'll keep that appointment I made for you. At the dentist. I'm working on something to protect you."

"Dad . . . wait—"

"All the things I've told you, pal. About **Belasko**. About Scarmarsh. About the **Superiors**. About all my adventures. I need you to forget as much as possible."

How? How was Hamish supposed to forget all that? It was *awesome!*

Dad opened his bag and brought something out.

It was a very small, very friendly-looking thing with a Belasko logo, big round eyes and a metal head. It made little chirruping sounds.

"This is a Hypnobit," said his dad. "I need you to look into its eyes."

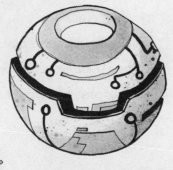

Hamish didn't understand, but did as his dad said.

And as he looked deeper into the robot's eyes, and as a light fragrant steam pumped out of four little holes on its metal forehead, Hamish felt sleepier and sleepier as he listened to his dad's voice. . .

Just before seven p.m., Hamish woke up on his bed.

A good job he did, too, because wasn't there something he was supposed to do this evening?

Oh, yeah! *Star Wars* with Dad!

He bound down the stairs, thrilled.

"I fell asleep!" he yelled, excitedly. "Hey Jimmy are we gonna watch *Star Wars?*"

Dad was in the kitchen with Mum. He was cuddling her and telling her she was the best, and she was laughing and cuddling him back and saying he was silly.

Hamish rubbed his eyes. Man, he was tired. How long had been asleep?! That was the problem with Christmas. It was over before you knew it. Seemed like only minutes ago they'd all been walking to the school hall to sing that awful song!

Hey, look – he was wearing Dad's Explorer. He'd forgotten about that present.

"Yo, bro," said Jimmy, giving him a hug as he settled down on the sofa next to him. "Sorry I didn't get you the telescope you wanted."

"Sorry that you stink," said Hamish, laughing, as Jimmy ruffled his hair.

Some people don't like it when life is just normal. Hamish did, though.

"I'm just popping out," said Dad, grabbing the car keys from the bowl by the window. "I'll get us some crisps and

ice cream."

The boys cheered at this. They looked up at their dad in the doorway.

"Love you, Dad," they said.

"Love you, boys," said Dad.

And Hamish and Jimmy sat there on the sofa, cuddled up with Mum, as the door gently closed, and the sound of Dad's car began to fade into the night.

SCRATCH TUFT and MOLE STUNK'S EPIC CHRISTMAS LIST

We want CHOCOLATE!
We want CHOCOLATE CATAPULTS!
We want CHOCOLATE CATAPULTS
THAT FIRE CHOCOLATE COINS!
We want CHOCOLATE CATAPULTS
THAT FIRE GOLD CHOCOLATE
COINS!
We want CHOCOLATE CATAPULTS
THAT FIRE GOLD CHOCOLATE
COINS THAT TURN INTO REAL.
COINS!
Actually it turns out we just want
coins.
JUST COINS PLEASE!

JIMMY'S NEW YEAR'S RESOLUTIONS

I know bad words are wrong and so next year I will NOT call Hamish. . .

A blinkin' NOODLEBEAR

A rummaging PICKLE TINKER

A stinky BADGER

A lolloping DAISY bumper

NIGEL, Queen of Great Britain

. A chicken licker

A toasty lip tickler

Fluff Bumbler the Third

Das Burp, a.k.a. "the German Burp"

Yvonne Peckering, a 56-year-old barber from Nuneaton

Twerpy Twerpy Doo-Dah

@jimmyellerby

HAPPY CHRISTMAS I AM EATING PEAS

↰ ↻0 ★0

@jimmyellerby

IS ANYBODY ELSE EATING CHRISTMAS PEAS

↰ ↻0 ★0

@jimmyellerby   FOLLOW

PEAS LOOK LIKE LITTLE GREEN BOULDERS

↰ ↻0 ★0

@jimmyellerby   FOLLOW

EXCEPT ONLY TO ANTS

↰ ↻0 ★0

@jimmyellerby

THEY LOOK LIKE BOULDERS THAT HAVE GONE OFF!

↰ ↻0 ★0

@jimmyellerby   FOLLOW

THEY LOOK LIKE BOULDERS THAT HAVE GONE OFF!

↰ ↻0 ★0

@jimmyellerby

IS THIS THING ON?

↰ ↻0 ★0

Clover's Christmas Cracker Joke

Q. Why won't Elliot light candles at Christmas?

A. Elf and safety!

ND PROUD OF

POS

Price

THE STARKLEY SONG I A CHRISTMAS NUMBE ONE!

Ernest Longblather, teacher and composer of the Starkley Song, was said to be "absolutely delighted" to learn that his song shot to number one in the charts yesterday!

"It is actually the only CD we sell in the Post Office," said the postmaster, Tubitha Bile, "so it is not surprising it went to number one."

One copy of the CD was sold yesterday, powering the Starkley Song straight to the top of Ms Biles's "World Music' chart, which also included a set of panpipes and a hat said to have belonged to Bavarian jazz singer Günther Schildkröte.

The Starkley Post managed to track down the mystery buyer whose purchase sent the song straight to the top spot – a certain Ernest Longblather himself!

"I'm so pleased to have made history with purchase," he said. "It really lovely to see p "get' my music."

So far, of cours remains the only per have got his music.

Merry Christmas Longblather!

The Golden Voice of
Ernest Longblather

The Starkley Song

THE TOOTH HURTS

Thinking of eating too many sweets at Christmas? Why not get ahead of the game? Come and get a tooth extracted, nice and early! We'll even take another one out for free!

**Christma Deal!
2-for-1
Extraction**

MEMO

Scarmarsh Industries Ltd, Isle of Frykt

To: All Terribles

Re: Christmas Dress

FOR ONE HOUR THIS CHRISTMAS YOU WILL BE PERMITTED A BRIEF PERIOD OF CELEBRATION.

You may hang Christmas baubles from your spikes or talons BUT THESE MUST BE SPIKY AND TREACHEROUS.

Ceremonial squeezing of pustules will begin as you eat lunch.

You may wear an elf or Santa hat, BUT THIS MUST BE FILTHY AND USED TO WIPE UP YOUR OWN SLIME.

You may hand ONE PRESENT to an associate of your choice, provided this present is an appropriate gift – for example, a bowl of dog hair.

SINGING must be done LOUDLY, OUT OF TUNE and TWO INCHES from the ear of a colleague.

Axel

P.S. Christmas Crackers will be available from reception. Please be aware they have been filled with 64 megagrams of highly volatile TNT.

ELLIOT AND
THE SUGAR RUSH

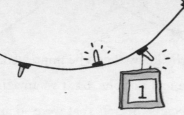

1

A Stranger Calls

There were 1,209 things Madame Cous Cous loved about Christmas.

Here was a woman who made a real effort this time of year.

She certainly made an effort in the way she dressed. From December 1st, she would thread fairy lights in her hair and wear star-shaped glasses. She'd wear a scarf made of tinsel too. Essentially, she looked like a human Christmas tree, which was fantastic, because not only did she look totally Christmassey, but she also saved money on buying a tree. (Although with all those fairy lights, she always had to make sure she was near a plug socket.)

Brilliantly, her entire shop – Madame Cous Cous's International World of Treats – would transform overnight into a Christmas wonderland. Starkley loved it. The whole town was excited to see what Madame Cous Cous's yuletide imagination had come up with every year.

Well, this Christmas she knew they'd be impressed.

Especially because she had not one, but two amazing and incredible Christmas secrets. Secrets that were so amazing and incredible that the woman could barely stop giggling. She had even hired a lawyer to make her sign a **"Don't Tell!"** contract so she didn't spill the Christmas beans ahead of December 1st.

The first secret was in the backyard of her shop. Madame Cous Cous was keeping something very special there. A little something she knew would delight each and every kid who came to visit. Something she had borrowed from an old friend in Lapland.

It was a *reindeer* called Captain Stanley Briggs! And what could be more Christmassy than a real life reindeer?

The second secret was the window of her shop.

Every year Madame Cous Cous's window had a different theme.

TWO YEARS AGO: "CHRISTMAS CAROLS" – featuring lots of different women called "Carol" covered in baubles.

Madame Cous Cous presents

Opening night!

Christmas Carols

LAST YEAR: "T'WAS THE BITE BEFORE CHRISTMAS!" – featuring an entire window display filled with fleas, spiders, rats, and other things that BITE. (This was widely accepted to be the worst Christmas display Madame Cous Cous or anyone else in the world had ever done.)

Madame Cous Cous presents

Opening night!

T'Was the Bite Before Christmas!

This year, Madame Cous Cous was very pleased with her theme. . .

REVENGE OF THE VIKING SANTAS!

Now, I know what you're thinking. A Viking Santa theme is a bit obvious, isn't it?

But this one was so intricate and so brilliant that Madame Cous Cous had swapped her normal glasses for huge, massive magnifying glasses so she could get every little detail right.

She'd crafted a ginormous longboat out of chocolate bars

and given it sails made from strawberry laces and huge sheets of liquorice. To stand alongside the boat, she'd made chocolate Vikings, all of which had cheery Santa hats and big pink beards made from candy floss. Each Viking held a very powerful sword made of toffee. This window was her Christmas masterpiece!

Just as she was working on a Polo-mint life vest, Madame Cous Cous heard the tinkle of the bell above her door and turned round. There in front of her stood the

HUGEST, BIGGEST MAN she'd

EVER SEEN in her LIFE!

She screamed at the SIZE of him!

How did he even FIT in here?!

Then she remembered she was still wearing her magnifying glasses.

When she took them off, she saw a short, round gentleman with an eye patch, elegantly holding a mahogany box. Her heart sank. She knew exactly what was happening, and she didn't like it. For this was a salesman. And what do salespeople do? They try and sell you something. That's literally how they got their name.

Madame Cous Cous hated it when people tried to sell her things. It didn't matter what those things were.

Encyclopaedias. Giant Siberian hamsters. Rectangular marbles. Avocados stuffed with socks. If it seemed like someone was going to give her the hard sell, it was always a big NO THANK YOU, because she was sure they'd try and rip her off. It was the reason she always kept a stick and a pair of running shoes nearby. You could often see Madame Cous Cous running salesmen out of town, huffing and puffing and whirling her stick above her head as they screamed and pounded away from Starkley.

It was a matter of pride, you see.

Madame Cous Cous prided herself on filling her entire sweet shop with treasures she'd hunted herself. Only then could she vouch for the quality. Off she'd pop to Botswana for the day to negotiate a deal for the very best Gabarone Gumballs. Maybe she'd swing by Luxembourg on the way home to convince the prime minister to part with a bottle of Deluxembourg Banana Mustards. Her life's work was a mission she took seriously, and she'd already bought all the stock for this Christmas, because she knew precisely what the children of Starkley liked to munch on.

So, no, she did not need salesmen. Not. At. All.

But there was something different about this one.

He was wearing a white lab coat over a check suit and he was

stroking the mahogany box like it was a very precious kitten.

"Let me tell you about the very latest technological breakthroughs in taste!" he said, in a very impressive French accent.

"What are you talking about?" barked Madame Cous Cous. "There haven't been any technological advancements in taste! Something either tastes of something or it doesn't!"

The man smiled a slow, creeping smile then waggled his finger.

"No, no," he said, two red cheeks wobbling as he shook his head. "For now I can reveal the latest in French delicacies, straight from Paris . . . the *bonbons superiors!*"

He opened the small wooden box slowly. And as he did, it trembled. White smoke started to billow from the edges. This was quite the special effect!

But Madame Cous Cous was not easily wowed. "I think your sweets are on fire," said Madame Cous Cous, waving the smoke away and coughing.

"That is not smoke, Madame," said the man, wafting it away by wiggling his eye patch. "This . . . is *sugar dust!*"

And as the box opened further and the dust cleared, Madame Cous Cous could just about make out three perfectly white spheres.

"You appear to be trying to sell me ping pong balls," she said. "Get out!"

"No, no, Madame! These are the perfect Christmas treat! You must try!"

The man – who hadn't yet told her his name or where he was from – plucked a ball from the box and held it towards her between two thin, wormy fingers.

"What are they called?" she said, holding one uncertainly.

"They are called **Sugar Poffs**," he said.

"Sugar Puffs?"

"Poffs," he said. "For why, you will see. Please, bite!"

And so very slowly, Madame Cous Cous raised the **Sugar Poff** to her lips. It was slightly squidgy, like a very firm marshmallow, but it felt strangely like sandpaper. It was heavy, and wobbled a bit in your hand, as if it had liquid in it. Also, it smelled of strawberries.

No, cola.

No, cherries!

And cakes and chocolate and gummy bears!

And when her two front teeth had only just pierced the outside. . .

POFF!

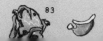

A cloud of sugar poffed around Madame Cous Cous's face . . . it rose into the air, twinkling and shining like a million little stars. The sugar danced around her hair, and merged with it, giving her barnet a silvery sparkle.

Madame Cous Cous couldn't say anything yet. She was still rolling the Sugar Poff around in her mouth, trying it, tasting it, teasing it, testing it. . .

"Well? What do you think, Madame?" said the salesman, grinning confidently and bringing out an order form he'd kept hidden in his sleeve.

And as Madame Cous Cous swallowed, her eyes suddenly seemed to grow to the size of watermelons.

And her nostrils flared.

And she stood on her tiptoes.

And her fingers tingled and tangled and tongled and bongled and her eyebrows shot straight to the very top of her forehead!

"I'LL TAKE EVERY LAST ONE OF THEM!" she screamed.

Cheese, Please!

"Hmm," said Elliot, looking up from his schoolwork at home. "I just don't know, Mum."

Mrs Elliot's face fell. She wanted her son to be excited by her Christmas shopping list, but young Elliot Elliot found it hard to be excited by things like Christmas shopping lists. He found other things exciting – like spores, moulds and fungus. But then we all find spores, moulds and fungus exciting, don't we?

"Elliot, Christmas is the one time of year you can eat anything you want!" said Mrs Elliot, willing him to be enthusiastic as she held her list aloft. "It's the time of year when eating your five-a-day means eating five sweets a day! Toffee Tambourines! Sweet 'n' Sour Scotch Eggs! Anything!"

But the fact was, Elliot was a savoury kid. He was nuts about nuts. Crackers about crackers. Totally carrots about carrots! He'd recently been getting into quinoa, but he never asked for any, because he didn't know how to pronounce it.

Hey – nor do *you*!

Good – me neither!

Elliot's friends in the **PDF** would have freaked out at the chance to have whatever treats they wanted for the Christmas season. He knew Hamish would have ordered a year's supply of Chomps, given half the chance. Hamish was brilliant. Elliot thought that if their lives were films, Hamish would be the action movie star who was HUGE on the posters and got to race about doing fun stuff. Elliot was more of a behind-the-scenes guy. A *thinking*, rather than *doing* guy. He was an athlete of the mind! Mostly he was fine with that, but sometimes, secretly, Elliot wished his friends would think *he'd* make a good action movie star. Even if the truth was that he could hardly even throw.

"Maybe just a cheese lollipop?" said Elliot, trying to make his mum happy. Christmas was the one time of year when she really let rip. Like his dad, Elliot's mum was a lecturer in antique leather shoe design and rather mild-mannered. This was a woman who enjoyed order every bit as much as Elliot. She always made sure Elliot arranged their ornaments in order of size. Books were to be arranged in alphabetical order. She always made sure Elliot had his five servings of fruit and vegetables per day, delivered in order of vitamin content. If she could have ordered more order, she'd have given orders to order! But at Christmas? Things were a little more relaxed. And a lot more sugary.

Just once, though, Elliot would have loved a totally *savoury* Christmas. Just once! But the fact was, Starkley just went sugar-loopy at Christmas. Anyway, that didn't matter, because right now, what Elliot wanted most was to get back to his school project on "The History of Leaves in France".

Elliot (**PDF** Codename: Brainbox) loved school projects. They gave him the chance to learn as much as possible at his own pace. Sometimes he'd do school projects even if the school hadn't asked him to. So far this year he'd handed in four voluntary projects including "The Five Best Train Timetables in Britain" and "Morse Code Using Just Spoons". He'd written an entire musical about felt called "Felt!" and he liked to joke that this was his best material.

His poor teacher, Mr Longblather, had to pretend he was thrilled every time a new three-hundred-page project landed on his desk, because that's what teachers are supposed to do. In reality, Ernest Longblather knew that every time Elliot Elliot handed in a new project, his entire weekend would be gone. There'd be no car boot sale in Thrupton for him. There'd be no Sunday afternoon sitting on his long brown sofa, bingeing on episodes of *Fast Cars Quickly*. No. He'd be reading up on "How to Spot the Moon Using Just Your Ears" or "The Twelve Best Ways to Tickle a Bumblebee". All signed off with Elliot's usual signature. (Elliot never wrote "by Elliot Elliot" at the end. He wrote "by Elliot²", so as to save time.)

"Just buy whatever you feel is right, Mum," he said, trying to get back to his important work, but noticing that outside the window, there was a right old kerfuffle of a kerfuffle. He watched as Hamish whizzed past on his scooter, yelling,

"Come on!"

Followed by Alice, shouting, **"Coming!"**

Then Buster a moment later, shouting, **"What?"**

Then Clover, shouting, "I think he said, "Come on!""

Then some of the other kids from the neighbourhood. Grenville Bile zoomed by on his BMX. Scratch Tuft and Mole Stunk on their rollerblades. And an old man being dragged by a dog.

French leaves were going to have to wait. Something was going on in Starkley.

Elf and Safety

Elliot skidded his scooter to a halt outside Madame Cous Cous's International World of Treats and leapt off!

Actually, that wasn't true. This was Elliot, after all.

He slowed his scooter to a controlled stop. Then carefully dismounted and took off his Christmas elf helmet. And unstrapped his knee protectors. And his elbow pads, shin pads and chin guard. Then made a note in his pad of the distance he had travelled and the likely wear this would have had on his tyres.

Elliot found himself in a growing crowd of kids and grown-ups, all chattering excitedly. Apparently, a rumour had gone around that Madame Cous Cous had totally lost it and was giving away her entire shop!

Outside the shop, Elliot spotted a big yellow rubbish skip outside the shop that had various sweets piled inside, as well as what looked like a giant chocolate longboat. Grenville

Bile's legs were poking out of the skip as he munched his way through the mainsail, like a dog devouring a steak. Scratch and Mole jumped in after him and started gobbling down tiny chocolate Vikings and shuddering in utter delight.

"Here!" yelled Madame Cous Cous, kicking open the door of her shop and swinging crates of sweets onto the street. She looked crazed as they crashed and clattered all over the place. Her hair was even more bedraggled than usual. Her eyes were bulging. She was moving so quickly she seemed almost like a blur.

"Take whatever you want!" she

screeched, as jelly beans bounced and plopped down drains and she pointed up to the heavens. "For I have found a miracle! A Christmas miracle!"

"What's going on?" said Elliot, finding his pals.

"She's gone mad," said Alice.

"She's thrown out her window display," Hamish added, pointing at the skip, "and brought the shutters down on the shop!"

"Why?" said Elliot, frowning.

"BEHOLD!" shouted Madame Cous Cous. **"My new Christmas window display!"**

The old lady pressed a button in the doorway and the big metal shutters began to judder and rise. Everyone watched in awe, waiting to see what would be revealed. What would this year's window display be? But the only thing in the window was row upon row of perfectly round white sweets. No tinsel. No fairy lights. Nothing saying, "MERRY CHRISTMAS". Just box after box of these plain and boring white balls. Case after case. Shelf upon shelf. Lit by so many spotlights and desk lamps they seemed almost to glow. And above them all a very fancy sign saying,

Les Bonbons Superiors!

"The greatest Christmas candies known to humankind!" said Madame Cous Cous. "The sweetest, tastiest, sugariest, most delicious-iest sweets in the world! So gorgeous and moreish you'll never want to eat anything else!"

The crowd began to salivate wildly. Grenville literally had

trails of spittle dangling from his cake-hole like stalagtites. No one had ever seen Madame Cous Cous so excited by a single sweet before.

"At last, my quest to seek out the world's best confectionary is over! My life's work is complete! Never again will I have to leave Starkley! For now we have – " she took a deep breath and smiled broadly as she held up a packet of –

"Sugar Poffs!"

Huh? What were **Sugar Poffs**? But, Elliot thought, even if they looked quite plain, if Madame Cous Cous said this was a Christmas miracle then a Christmas miracle it must surely be.

Mr Longblather said, "Um, well, I'll take two packs!"

And Old Mr Neate said, "Go on, then, me too!"

And then the kids started rifling through their pockets to find loose change and suddenly there was a rush for the doors because no one wanted to be last in line and miss out.

"Well, I guess they must be good, if you like that sort of thing," shrugged Elliot, looking to his friends.

Hamish and Alice had already bolted for the door to make sure they got their fair share of whatever these amazing new sweets might be.

Elliot stayed put as the relentless TING! of Madame Cous

Cous's till filled the air. Kids and grown-ups were squashed in the doorway of **International World of Treats** as the window display got smaller and smaller. Every now and again you'd see Madame Cous Cous's stick hooking another pack of **Sugar Poffs** to sell to an eager customer.

Eventually, Hamish and Alice bounded outside, followed by Clover, Buster and Venk. Each one held a packet of **Sugar Poffs**.

"Want one?" asked Buster.

"Not really my thing," said Elliot.

"What, not even at Christmas?" said Hamish. "Well, more for us, then!"

"What are they even supposed to taste of?" asked Elliot.

"Only one way to find out!" said Clover. "It's not rocket science!"

So she very carefully held one to her mouth and bit into it. **POFF!**

And you'll never guess what happened next.

Don't Sweet It!

Elliot had never seen anything like it.

Such glee! Such excitement! Such insane, crazy, NUTTY happiness!

"OH! MY! WORD!" Clover yelled, as sugar dust twinkled around her head and landed on her cheeks like glitter. **"THESE! ARE! AWESOME!"**

POFF!

Another burst of sugar dust exploded as Hamish bit into his sweet.

"WAHOOOO!" he shouted, and Alice immediately bit into hers.

POFF!

POFF! POFF! POFF!

There were so many people biting into so many Sugar Poffs that the sugar dust was almost coating the town square! It snaked into the air and twirled above everyone's heads. It moved with the breeze, dusting the wintery branches of the bare trees like frost and settling on the ground.

"Let's make Sugar Angels!" squealed Clover, lying flat on her back and flapping her arms up and down on the pavement in glee.

As more and more people bit into the Poffs, the dust all around them caught the cold December sunshine. For a second it looked like a crazy outdoor disco, Elliot thought. And not just because of the strange sugary smoke. Because of what people were doing!

Elliot watched in confusion as people around him began shaking.

And shuddering.

And dancing with enormous grins on their big silly faces!

They just couldn't stop moving. One lady had started breakdancing on a car. Mr Slackjaw was skipping. Old Mr Neate was furiously clapping at a tree. Frau Fussbundler had taken off her skirt and was waving it above her head! Clover was doing a dance called the Robot. Or as she'd call it, the Clo-bot.

Elliot had never seen such joy, and couldn't help but smile.

People were high-fiving and jumping from foot to foot. Some of them were running around in circles, like cats chasing their tails. And Madame Cous Cous stood at the window, watching proudly.

People were so excited and so full of beans. Everyone kept coming up with amazing plans.

"We should build a massive zip wire!" said the policeman, PC Wix, to no one in particular. "We could all travel about on zip wires! Starkley could become the first TOTALLY ZIP-WIRED TOWN IN THE WORLD!"

"Who wants to start a nursery for dogs?" yelled Frau Fussbundler.

"I'm going to run a marathon!" screeched Grenville Bile, and that was when Elliot started to think that the something must be up.

These Sugar Poffs must be incredible, if everyone was having such a reaction!

"Okay, maybe I will try one," he said to his friends, feeling a little left out. He reached out his hand and was shocked when his friends all jumped away from him.

"You should go and get your own," said Venk, clutching his packet to his chest.

"Can't I have one of yours?" said Elliot.

"Er, I need all mine," said Venk.

This was weird. The PDF shared everything. They were

best friends.

"I didn't bring any money with me," said Elliot.

He turned to Alice, surely she would give him one of hers? Alice was the best.

But Alice had gone all bug-eyed and loopy. She took out her second Sugar Poff and instead of offering it to Elliot, POFF!

"I'm going to build a rocket and fly to Hungary!" she cried.

"Hamish? Could I have one? Just one?" Elliot asked.

Hamish was too engrossed in his Sugar Poffs packet to hear. He had turned his packet inside out and was licking it.

Elliot was surprised. This wasn't like his pals at all.

He took a step back and cast his eye around the square. The sound of excited chitter-chatter was deafening.

Everyone was talking, but no one was *listening*.

As his eyes looked higher, he saw that far above them, a cloud was gathering.

A twinkling, silvery cloud. A cloud of purest sugar.

And as the wind rose, the cloud began to thin and spread out . . . all over Starkley.

What's Wrong, Sugar?

Elliot had gone from really wanting to try a Sugar Poff to not wanting them at all.

There was something about them that seemed to make people lose control. Losing control did not appeal to Elliot one bit.

One child to his right was crossing out everything on his Christmas list and writing **Sugar Poffs! Sugar Poffs! Sugar Poffs!** over and over again. Another kid bit into two Sugar Poffs at once and made a blissful face as sugar dust POFFed out of her ears! Mr Longblather was acting very strangely indeed. He kept running into a tree, getting up, dusting himself off, and running into the tree again. Elliot couldn't help but wonder if this crazy feeling in the air was actually something to do with all the sugar in the air. Sugar he'd watched start to spread . . .

"MAKE WAY AT ONCE!" shouted a familiar voice from behind him.

He whirled round to see his mum striding towards him with his dad at her side. They were at the front of a big crowd of grown-ups who were stamping towards the sweet shop from the far edges of town. Phew! They were obviously here to stop everyone acting so bizarrely!

"Mum! Dad!" said Elliot, but they thundered straight past him. Elliot was jostled around as more kids and teachers, and even passing taxi drivers, ran to join a long and snaking queue, which seemed to trail all the way to the neighbouring town of Frinkley. Even his parents had been sucked into the sugar frenzy! The **TING TING TING** of Madame Cous Cous's till rang far and wide. All around the square, cars were honking their horns as people tried to find parking spaces. Bike racks were filling up. And the bins were jam-packed with Sugar Poff wrappings.

Chaos!

Madame Cous Cous was delighted, though. She'd never done such a roaring trade. For years her shop had stood in Starkley, proudly serving the children of the town, but now it felt like Starkley *was* International World of

Treats. Like the store was the very centre of the universe!

"From now on, all postcards of Starkley will just be pictures of this shop!" proclaimed the mayor, who could *not* stop jiggling as he POFFed.

And throughout all this madness, Elliot stood to one side, watching his friends line up for more, not sure how to feel.

On the one hand, he was a bit jealous that he was missing out, but on the other, he had the distinct feeling that something very wrong was happening. His mum and dad didn't even seem to be looking for him. And he felt a bit frustrated that his friends were suddenly behaving so childishly. And the grown-ups too!

HOOOONK!
HOOOONK!

He was jolted from his thoughts by the sound of a giant truck's horn, and felt the ground vibrate as it rumbled into the square.

"*L.B.S.!*" said the writing on the side.

The great lorry hissed and jolted to a stop. A moment later, a strange man wearing an eye patch opened the back doors.

"More Sugar Poffs are here!" shouted Mr Longblather, slamming into that tree again, then getting up and padding towards the truck.

"It's my second delivery from L.B.S.!" shouted Madame Cous Cous, and the whole town cheered.

Elliot was the only person not looking at the sweets in the back of the truck. No, Elliot was looking at the man wearing the eye patch. The expression on the man's face was a little odd. He was smiling, but it was a strange smile.

It wasn't a generous smile. It wasn't a smile that said, "I'm pleased you all like my sweets." It was a smile that said, "Of course you like my sweets."

It was an *arrogant* smile. And Elliot didn't like it one bit.

Elliot noticed the man was wearing a small orange badge that said, "I BEAT THE BADGER'S BURGER!" and on the truck's dashboard, just under a Pay 'n' Display ticket from a car park not far away, there was a packet of half-eaten chips. Elliot thought it was strange that if these sweets had only just been delivered, the salesman would have been hanging around nearby scoffing fat chips. Surely the second he'd sold his sweets to Starkley he'd have gone straight to the next town? Why had he been hanging around?

"HERE!" shouted Madame Cous Cous, from behind the truck. **"GRAB THIS!"**

She was chucking out crates of Sugar Poffs and taking people's money hand over fist. People weren't just buying packets now – they were buying whole boxes!

Elliot stared in disbelief as the crowd began to scrabble against each other, pushing each other out of the way. He was so confused he had to clean his glasses to make sure he was seeing what he was seeing. What happened to queueing, or waiting your turn? What happened to children going

first? Even his own mother was trying to trip his father up so that she could get her hands on them before he did.

One crate fell to the ground in the scuffle, bursting open and sending **Sugar Poffs** bouncing down the road. People screamed. Grenville Bile ran after them, chased closely by Clover and Buster, a pensioner on a mobility scooter and six slathering members of the Starkley Women's Institute. They leapt and dove for them, crashing together in a big heap and slapping at each others' wrists as they tried to scoop them up. It looked like a real-life game of Hungry Hippos.

Just then, something rolled and tapped against Elliot's shoe. He looked down.

A **Sugar Poff.**

6

Sweet 'n' Power

Elliot pinned the diagram he'd just drawn to the wall of the **WAR ROOM** he'd made in the shed at the bottom of his garden. This was where he undertook important research on behalf of the **PDF**. It was packed with posters of their enemies, To Do lists and scientific equipment.

He decided maybe he'd just study the Sugar Poff under his microscope one last time to be completely certain.

It was evening now and quiet outside. The winter air was colder. Ever-larger lumps of sugar dust were falling from the sky, like strange snowfall, coating the streets. Someone had started to build a snowman from sugar on his street, but abandoned it halfway through, presumably to run off to buy more Sugar Poffs. As he worked, he could hear small thumps on his roof as sugar-clumps fell to Earth, around streets that were empty and quiet.

Elliot clicked his yellow desk lamp on. He was surrounded by all the tools of his trade. Protractors. Compasses. Pencils. A tiny statue of Einstein doing a skydive.

His tummy rumbled. He was just about the only person in Starkley who hadn't filled up on sweets today. His parents seemed to have forgotten all about dinner. Even though it was Elliot's tofu and aubergine stir fry night. It was his signature dish. Not that the PDF would ever have eaten it. They preferred sausage and chips round Hamish's house. But Elliot's mum and dad loved his creations. The last time Elliot had seen his parents, though, they were running around in circles in Christmas hats in the town square. He guessed that's what they were still doing.

He could hear the distant POFFS POFFING away and see the sugar strands twirling through the air outside. In the past hour or so, he had at least identified the sweet's main components, as shown in his super-detailed diagram.

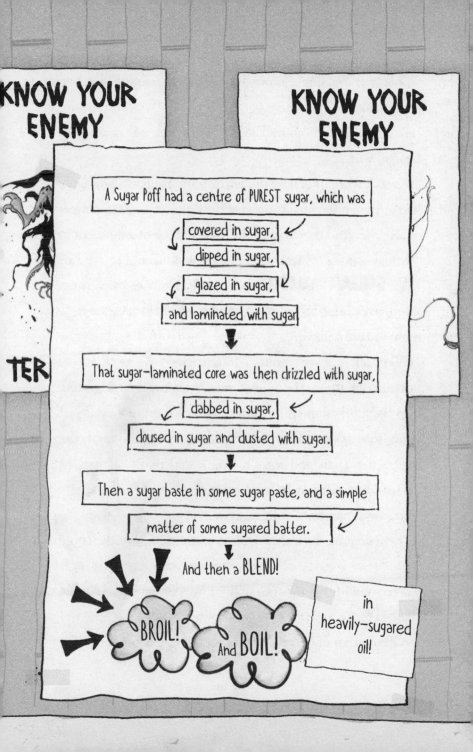

This was the single most sophisticated sweet Elliot had ever seen.

All that sugar, thought Elliot, *packed into one sandpapery sugary shell!*

It was a work of art, really. Technically brilliant. Someone had obviously decided to aim for the sickliest, sugariest sweet of all time. And they had created something of a moment in Starkley's unusual history: a . . . well, what would you call it?

A SUGAR RUSH! thought Elliot. *One that swept through the whole town.* **A SUGAR RUSH** *so powerful it caused a rush to sugar!*

Elliot felt uneasy about a single sweet being quite so potent. But if everybody else was having fun, and getting into the Christmas spirit, he wondered whether he was just being too serious about things. As he made his way down the garden path and into his dark and empty house, he decided he must just be over-reacting.

I mean, it had to be fun, right?

There couldn't be a downside to such a big upside, could there?

What could be the possible downside of a **SUGAR RUSH?**

With no sign of Mum or Dad coming home just yet, Elliot

found himself a plate of cold vegetables and was just about
to head upstairs to his room when . . . WHAT?

The phone rang.

7

Candy Chaos!

By the time Elliot scooted back to the town square, things had got way worse.

Like – *way* worse.

His mum had sounded pretty panicky on the phone.

"Madame Cous Cous has run out of **Sugar Poffs!**" she'd shouted, and in the background all Elliot could hear was crazed yelling and sirens.

"Come home, then!" he'd said. "It's my tofu and aubergine stir fry night! And *Britain's Brainiest Boffins and Brainboxes* is on telly! And you said you'd give me a short lecture on what langoustines are!"

His mum had laughed maniacally, like having a stir fry and watching telly and talking about posh names for shellfish was the most insane thing anyone had ever suggested. Because it *was*, when there were **Sugar Poffs** to be had!

"We need to start bargaining with people!" she'd said. "Sweetpea, bring some of our treasures! For tonight we will swap them for sugared French goods!"

Elliot wasn't used to his mum being so weird. And he hadn't been able to work out what his family's treasures were, so he'd just brought an old vase that had belonged to his grandma and his mum's purse.

As he looked around, Elliot could not believe his eyes.

What had *happened* in the last couple of hours?

The town square had been such a happy place when he'd left it. But now people were going nuts. They were bug-eyed and drooling, clutching each other and asking who had more **Sugar Poffs!** He looked around, trying to spot his friends.

There were people on roofs, shaking chimneys.

There were people searching exhaust pipes, and people tapping drainpipes.

There were people everywhere, jibbering and jabbering and desperately trying to locate more of the eye-patch man's candies.

PC Wix was moving from person to person, saying, "I am a policeman and I demand you hand over any **Sugar Poffs** you might have about your person!" But PC Wix had lost

111

rather a lot of his authority since the sugar rush had made him think it was a good idea to swap his trousers for a tutu.

"Sweetpea! Good!" said Elliot's mum, appearing as if from nowhere and grabbing the vase from his hands with her trembling hands, before turning away and shouting: "Who will swap one Sugar Poff for this priceless old vase?"

"Mum! Just come home!" he pleaded. "They're just sweets!"

"They are NOT just SWEETS, boy!" said his dad, who suddenly had a black eye and whose hair was all over the place. "They are SUGAR POFFS!"

His dad didn't seem like his dad any more. Dad's idea of a good time was to sit quietly in a room on his own. But this new version of Dad? He seemed wild and dangerous and like he might suddenly do something CRAZY, like get a tattoo or kiss a parrot or push a nun in a lake.

Elliot realized what was happening. The sugar rush was wearing off, and people were panicking as they felt it disappear. Now he understood why Mr Slackjaw was quickly licking forty-three lollypops he'd gaffer-taped together to create what he called a *Jolly*-pop.

He had to find his friends. They would doubtless have noticed this too!

But there, look!

Clover was standing outside Lord of the Fries dressed as a matador and chugging down two-litre bottles of Quirky Cola.

Buster had whizzed his ice-cream van round – and the rest of the PDF were lying under the ice cream nozzle as he filled their gobs with custard fudge ice cream!

The whole town was trying to keep the sugar rush going – even his friends!

"Hamish!" said Elliot, trying to jump up to the window where they could see him. "Alice! You need to snap out of this!"

But even as he said it, he knew they were just too far gone. They were obsessed with sugar. Possessed by it. Their faces were smudged with liquorice. Their fingers were marked by aniseed and chocolate and whatever else they'd tried to get their grubby little hands on to try and stay chock-full of sugar.

Well, thought Elliot. *As far as plans go, we obviously have to get more* Sugar Poffs.

This was a *terrible* plan. What was he thinking?

He looked around for Madame Cous Cous and saw her standing in the doorway of the **International World of Treats,** cowering in the shadows, stepping slowly backwards.

Her shelves were bare.

Her entire stock was gone. Even the skip had been licked clean!

And Madame Cous Cous looked frightened.

People had turned **International World of Treats** upside-down trying to trace any lost or hidden Sugar Poffs. This **SUGAR RUSH** had spiralled out of control and taken a dark turn.

Elliot ran to the doorway, and managed to jam his foot inside just as the old lady tried to close her door.

"I haven't got any more!" she shouted. "He's not answering his phone! I told you people! *There are no more* Sugar Poffs."

Suddenly, from behind him, Elliot heard an enormous CRASH.

Some of the grown-ups had been shaking the Christmas tree that sat in the middle of the town square. They'd attacked it so fiercely in their raging sugar-anger that the tree had been pulled from its roots and thundered to the ground. The Christmas lights running from the tree all around the square like bunting, had snapped and collapsed, bucking and sparking on the floor like electric snakes.

"I don't want any Sugar Poffs, Madame Cous Cous!" shouted Elliot over the chaos. "I just want to work out how to stop all this!"

There was a pause as, hidden from view, Madame Cous Cous said nothing.

And then out came her stick.

It hooked around Elliot's neck and yanked him quickly inside.

8

I Predict a. . .

"RIOT! It's going to turn into a riot!" said Madame Cous Cous, peering nervously through a gap in the shutters. "It got out of hand so quickly!"

Outside, a bin had caught fire and two of Elliot's teachers were fighting over who'd get to sniff an empty Mars Bar wrapper. Grenville Bile's mum, the postmaster, had barged her way into a café and grabbed all the little sachets of sugar. She was pouring them straight into her gob while holding Grenville back with one enormous fist!

"Can't you just order more **Sugar Poffs?**" asked Elliot.

"Don't you think I've been trying?" Madame Cous Cous replied. "The Frenchman's stopped answering his phone! The *L.B.S.* website has disappeared too. It's like the whole thing was just made up! Like it was some kind of trick being played on us!"

Elliot put his hands on his hips. What kind of salesman would sell you something just so he could *not* sell it to you any more?

Wait . . . Only a salesman who knew what would happen when he stopped . . .

Only a salesman who *wanted* chaos to break out in Starkley!

Instinctively, Elliot wanted to run to the **PDF**. This was exactly the kind of situation that he and his pals would sort out together, but the problem was that the rest of the PDF were currently on their backs in an ice-cream van, out of their minds on custard fudge.

And if he opened that door he'd have to make his way through the crowds again. Things were turning nasty out there. This was not part of his skillset! Hamish was the action movie guy, but Hamish was up to the gills in sugar! So now it was down to Elliot to come up with a cunning plan to get people back to how they'd been. And not just come up with one – carry it out too. All on his own! Without Alice or Hamish!

But this was not a time for fear. This was a time for action.

"*L.B.S.*," he said urgently. "Did the salesman say what that stands for?"

"*Les Bonbons Superiors*," replied Madame Cous Cous.

"That's either French," said Elliot, drumming his fingers on his chin. "Or there is someone out there whose name is Les Bonbons."

"It's French," said Madame Cous Cous, who was fluent in French, what with being a Madame and all. "In fact, *Les Bonbons* **Superior** means "the *best* sweeties'. Or "the finest sweeties'. Or. . ."

"*Superior* sweeties," said Elliot.

His eyes became steely.

His breathing stopped.

There was something about that phrase.

That word.

That *one word*.

Superior.

"Madame Cous Cous!" said Elliot, alarmed. **"It's a plan against Starkley! It's an ATTACK by the SUPERIORS!"**

The old lady looked shocked. It had never ever occurred to her that the Superiors – that evil, alien race that had sent so much trouble to their town in the past – might be using her own goodwill and sense of Christmas spirit against Starkley.

"But why would they want to get everyone so excited? So happy?" she said.

"Because of what always follows a **SUGAR RUSH**..." said Elliot.

He was scaring even himself, his brain firing on all cylinders, as he worked out what the Superiors' plan must be.

"A **SUGAR RUSH** is followed by a **SUGAR CRASH**," said Elliot. "A complete depletion of energy! A lack of vitality! An era of laziness! That was the plan all along!"

"What was?" said Madame Cous Cous, still confused.

"The Superiors wanted us to use up all our energy so that we would become listless! We wouldn't have the energy to fight back or defend ourselves! We would be pushovers! Too tired and grumpy and lazy to do anything! The *bonbons* were sent here for a reason! The Superiors have prepared Starkley for an invasion!"

"Then we must do something!" said Madame Cous Cous. "Before this chaos continues!"

And as she said that, both Elliot and Madame Cous Cous realized something had changed.

Because in the moment of silence that followed, they knew – this was a moment of *silence*.

There was no shouting from outside. No fighting. No car horns or sirens.

Just nothing.

They turned to the window. Bright white light shone through the cracks and dust danced in the air around them, but they could sense no movement from outside. It was intimidatingly quiet.

Nervously, Madame Cous Cous pressed UP on the shutters to her shop.

And when those shutters rose, Elliot and Madame Cous Cous inhaled sharply and with some fear.

Standing at the window . . . *was the entire town of Starkley. Staring.*

Eyes half-open.

Eyebrows low.

Arms by their sides.

Drool slowly dripping from their mouths.

Hamish. Alice. Buster. Clover. Venk.

Elliot's mum and dad.

Mr Longblather, Grenville Bile, *everyone*.

The ones at the front were so out of it they were trying to walk into the shop but their heads just kept bumping at the window.

And all of them moaning.

Moaning like *zombies!*

Nom Nom Nombies!

"It's happened!" said Elliot, stepping slowly backwards through the room to try and avoid the dulled, lifeless eyes of these weirdo zombies. "That's the **SUGAR CRASH!**"

"I've never seen one so powerful!" said Madame Cous Cous. "Usually people just get a bit grumpy or tired! This is another level! It's turned them into . . . creatures of the night!"

BUUUUUUUUUUU came a loud, unified moan from outside.

"It's the **Sugar Poffs**," said Elliot. "So intensely sugary they've affected the whole town. Well, everyone except me and you."

"I have a very high tolerance to sugar," said Madame Cous Cous, shrugging. "I have been working surrounded by sugar dust for *many* years."

But Elliot knew they had a real problem here. If what he

suspected was true, then with the whole town completely zombified by a lack of sugar, it would be easy for the Superiors to move in and do whatever they wanted. This huge mob of groaning, moaning, energy-free citizens all crowding round the sweetshop was like one big advert for an invasion! Elliot imagined they might as well have been carrying placards...

Hey, Superiors!
Fancy taking out one of Belasko's top agents? Easy! He's standing right behind Hamish, trying to walk through a window!

Les Bonbons
Turns a Ze into a Ze

Hey, Superiors!
Fancy walking into Lord of the Fries and cooking all the sausages? Literally no one is in a position to stop you. Although do remember to cook them properly, because food poisoning is no laughing matter.

Les Bonbons Superiors!
Turns a Hero into a Zero!

Hey, Superiors!
Want to put an end to the PDF? Simple! They're all right here, with no energy and absolutely defenceless!

Les Bonbons Superiors!
Turns a Hero into a Zero!

Hey, Superiors!
Honestly, dudes, this is easy pickings. You wanna get down here. You'll love it!

Les Bonbons Superiors!
Turns a Hero into a Zero!

Just look at them!

All droopy and blank-eyed and shuffling slowly around!

Elliot spotted Hamish's brother, Jimmy. He'd managed to find the energy to slap one sweaty hand on the window, and now dragged it down the pane so that it made that awful noise that turns your knees all wobbly and your legs all soupy. Elliot would rather have heard anything than that noise! Even one of Jimmy's "poems". Jimmy was grunting but still had his phone in his other hand. Sometimes, it was very hard to tell the difference between a zombie and a normal fifteen-year-old.

And look!

The front door was rattling! The people outside wanted to get *in*side. And they were *creepy*. Elliot was only grateful that he wasn't made out of sugar, or he was sure they'd lick him until there was nothing left!

"I'm not sure how to get rid of a sugar crash," said Madame Cous Cous. "I only know about sugar rushes! Do we just wait?"

Elliot shook his head. With this amount of sugar in everyone's system, the crash could last weeks! They had to move swiftly if Starkley was to avoid big trouble. The Superiors would be watching for the crash to take hold, and then they would make their move. The last thing everyone needed was a bunch of super-intelligent awfuls like the Superiors taking over the town. They were always up to something; always plotting in the background. They were supposed to be leaving Starkley alone so that the town's real nemesis, Axel Scarmarsh, could one day claim it as his own. But maybe they were just too evil to stick to a deal. . .

Elliot knew he had to end this sugar crash and get everyone back on an even keel.

But how?

Elliot needed to be a one-man **PDF**, and a one-man **PDF** needed a brilliant plan.

He whipped out his notepad and began to write:

1. I have to get that sugar out of people's systems!

2. I have to replace that sugar with something else!

"Hmm. That sounds a little simplistic," said Madame Cous Cous, looking at Elliot's notes.

So Elliot added a couple more things:

1. I have to get that sugar out of people's systems!

2. I have to replace that sugar with something else!

3. I have to find that salesman!

4. I have to STOP THAT INVASION!

"Now *that*," said Madame Cous Cous, "sounds more like a plan."

Elliot knew precisely where he had to start. But as he looked at the door he saw the doorknob was still rattling. The window was still filled with zombified citizens as far as Elliot could see.

"A plan is all well and good, Madame Cous Cous," he said, turning and fixing her with an icy glare. "But I'm trapped. In a shop! Surrounded by zombies! How on *earth* am I going to get out of here?!"

10

Sweet Revenge!

"WAHOO!" yelled Elliot, clinging on for dear life as Captain Stanley Briggs the reindeer **SMASHED** through the door of **International World of Treats**, all hooves blazing!

They sent zombified sugar crashers flying as they pushed through the crowd of slow-moving oddbods, the reindeer using his antlers to prod and poke people out of the way.

"Go, Captain Briggs! Go!" said Elliot, hanging onto his glasses with one hand and trying to steer the reindeer with the other as the mighty beast broke into a gallop. They LEAPT over the fallen Christmas tree – and Elliot's heart leapt too!

This was the closest he had ever felt to being an action hero and he loved it! He was no longer just a thinking guy – Elliot^2 was a *doing* guy! Now all he had to do was work on his throwing!

The clatter of the reindeer's hooves on the concrete pavements of Starkley was completely thrilling. Captain Briggs was a big, proud animal with strong legs, a puffed chest and piercing eyes. He had the look of a *military* reindeer. Elliot could never have imagined he'd get the chance to actually ride an animal like this. And ride one on his very own mission!

Any sense of action hero glee he felt had to be put to one side, though. He had to focus! *Doing* without *thinking* was pointless. Elliot was sure that the salesman would still be around somewhere, making sure everyone had fallen under his sugar spell. But he wouldn't risk being seen in the middle of town. He'd be inundated by people desperate for Sugar Poffs. No, he'd keep himself *juuuust* far enough away.

And as Captain Briggs hurtled over a fence and thundered through a field – steered somehow by Elliot – the boy had a pretty good idea where.

"There," whispered Elliot, as he clambered off his Christmas steed and kept low behind a wall.

A few kilometres out of Starkley was Starkley Services.

It was a petrol station. But not just a petrol station. It also had a toilet.

Okay, it was not the most exciting place on Earth, unless you're reeeeeally into toilets. But just there, in the car park, Elliot could see the large truck with L.B.S.! on the side.

Aha! Elliot had been right! He'd *known* this must be where the salesman would be. How? Well, remember that orange, "I BEAT THE BADGER'S BURGER!" badge Elliot had noticed the salesman wearing? The only way to get one of those badges was to eat "The Full Badger" at Badger's Burgers. That meant a Badger's Big Beanburger, chips, chips, chips, chips and a chip-flavoured dip. And Badger's Burgers was right here at Starkley Services, alongside a small motel called the Roadway Inn.

That had to be where the salesmen was staying. The Roadway Inn had a gym in it, called InnAction. It also had a restaurant called InnEdible. Starkley Services was the *perfect* place for someone to hide out for a couple of days.

"You stay here," whispered Elliot to Captain Briggs as he took a deep breath and got ready to investigate.

His investigation had hardly begun when the door to Badger's Burgers tinkled open, and out walked the man in the eye patch, looking rather bloated and bilious. He was rubbing his tummy and had a brand new badge: "I BEAT THE BADGER'S CHRISTMAS BURGER!" He leaned against a wall and burped, regretting ever thinking a giant Brussels sprout in a bun would be a good idea for his dinner. As he gathered himself together, the chef from InnEdible walked out to the bins next to him to throw away a big sack of old fruit and vegetables.

Elliot tapped his chin, and whispered,

"I think I've got a plan, Captain Briggs."

Just Desserts!

Pester Grool the salesman was happy that he could finally knock off for the night.

In the morning, Starkley would have fallen. Everyone would be so tired out from the sugar crash that they would sleep long and hard. Then, when they woke up, Pester just had one thing left to do to make sure the townsfolk would be easy pickings for his superiors, the Superiors. He tried not to think too much about the innocent people who would be affected. The old people and the children. He was sure that once the Superiors had enslaved the people of Starkley they'd be kind enough to them. Sure, everyone would have to get used to eating nothing but watery porridge and going to school for twenty-three hours of every day and never being allowed sweets again, but Pester didn't like thinking about that kind of stuff. Instead he tried to focus on all the money he was getting paid for introducing these evil, laboratory-made Sugar Poffs to Starkley.

The Poffs were the product of hours of overtime from the **Terribles** – those awful monsters who lived on the island of Frykt. The ones developed by Scarmarsh. They had been carefully working out the perfect formula for just the right amount of sugar to create a HUGE rush and an even HUGER crash. In fact, several of their "tasters" in the Quality Control Department had eaten so many Sugar Poffs they'd simply exploded, showering the place with awful fatty chunks of nasty.

Pester stared up at the sky. If everything was going according to plan, he should just about be able to make out the Superiors' Spy Satellite, which would be on schedule to arrive about now. It would be up there, somewhere in the cosmos, waiting for his SOS.

Yes, the sooner he'd sent that SOS and was out of Starkley and back to France the better. He could get back to work on his pride and joy – Elisa, his canal boat.

BRRRRRRUUUUMMMMP.

Oof. That was his tummy. He really shouldn't eat giant burgers made of Brussels sprouts. To be honest, no one should.

BRRRRUUUUUUMMMP.

Maybe he should just get to bed. Or the toilet.

But as Pester rubbed his belly and tried not to burp too loudly, he stopped in his tracks.

Had he seen something moving about in the shadows? Just there, near his truck?

What was that?

He squinted into the darkness to see if he could get a better look.

CLA-BANK!

He turned, startled, to see a bin rocking from side to side! That was weird.

Perhaps it had been a cat? Or maybe the chef from InnEdible had thrown more old vegetables on the heap?

Pester stifled another Brussels-burp (or "brurp") and headed quickly to his room. He was getting a little creeped out and he wanted to get inside. As he fumbled for his room key, he heard a noise coming from the back of his lorry.

He knew immediately what had happened. Burglars! Someone who'd had a taste of **Sugar Poffs** and tracked him down. He knew he should have found somewhere further away to stay. Well, he'd teach this thief a lesson, all right.

Pester got himself ready for action. He flung the back door

open and LEAPT in!

"Stay where you are!" he screamed into the darkness.

What he heard was not what he was expecting to hear.

He heard a SNORT.

He heard HOOVES.

He felt hot, sour breath getting CLOSER.

He knew all about the **Terribles**. He knew about their links to Scarmarsh, and the Superiors. But he had never actually seen one. They were supposed to be DISGUSTING, with **CLAWS** and TALONS and DROOL galore. The very idea of them filled him with terror, even if technically he was on *their* side.

"Oh, no, oh, please, stop!" he cried, worried he'd never see his darling Elisa again. "Don't come any closer!"

But the hooves kept coming. . . the breath getting nearer. . .

He knew the Superiors wouldn't send a **Terrible** if it was good news. **Terribles** don't come to tell you that you've done a good job.

No, if someone sent you a **Terrible**, there was a terrible, terrible reason for that. But what had he done wrong?

Pester sank to his knees and stared upwards, scared witless, waiting for the creature to come to the light, waiting to see the face that stalked his nightmares. . .

When. . .

"HUH?"

He appeared to be staring straight at an enormous reindeer.

"What the—?"

"KEEP HIM THERE, Briggsy!" yelled a voice from behind him.

Pester spun round. *A kid?!*

And while Captain Briggs hooked the Frenchman with his antlers and flung him to the other side of the truck, Elliot slammed shut the doors and made a run for the driver's seat!

"Okay!" Elliot told himself as he clambered inside the cab of the lorry and hoisted up the big bags of fruit and vegetables he'd taken from the bins. "I can do this!"

All the action films he'd ever watched suggested that bad guys hid the keys to their vehicles on the little flappy sun visor at the front, so Elliot flipped it down.

No keys!

So he opened the glove compartment. There was a mahogany box in there. He grabbed it and flicked it open. The truck immediately began to fill with sugar dust.

"Yuk!" he said, wafting it away from the box, revealing two pristine **Sugar Poffs** – the leftovers of the salesman's samples! Elliot was sure they would come in handy later. . .

But right now he needed that key!

Elliot decided his only option was to do something extraordinary using just the paperclip he always kept in his left pocket. He was going to have to masterfully bend and straighten that paperclip until it formed a perfect key, and then using his skills and Belasko training he would manipulate inside the ignition of the truck, until bingo! He could start that engine!

And then he looked down at the ignition and saw that the keys were already in there.

"That works too," he said with a shrug. "Buckle up, Briggs! We're off to save Starkley!"

The truck ROARED into life.

Now, Elliot knew how to drive, thanks to a few lessons from Buster in his ice-cream van. But driving a truck all alone was actually quite a thrill, even though he was doing it without a helmet, or shin pads, knee pads and elbow pads.

As he sped down the country lane towards Starkley (taking care to stick to both regional and national speed limits), Elliot noticed something forming in the skies above him. It was like watching a strange cloud gather. A cloud that had begun as a sort of mist in the cosmos but was now almost solid. Was that . . . sugar?! He had no idea what it meant, but he had enough experience of odd things to know it couldn't be good.

He stepped on the brakes as he approached Starkley. He had to be careful. There could be slow-moving zombified sugar-crashers anywhere!

"Briggs! We're here!" he whisper-shouted to the back of the truck. "Get ready!"

As Elliot drove into the town square, he honked his horn loudly. Like slow meerkats, the dozens and dozens of sugar-crashers turned and stared at him.

"Look what I've got!" yelled Elliot, and he held out a Sugar Poff from the window so they could all see.

BUUUUUUUUUUUUUUUH! moaned the zombie townsfolk. Their mouths were wide open and they began plodding clumsily towards his outstretched hand.

He could see Hamish stomping his way forwards, his face all blank and drooling. Alice was behind him, and Clover too, both drenched in ice cream. Elliot kept his foot gently on the accelerator, moving the truck very slowly. His plan was to get them all to follow him.

Where? He had no idea.

Why? Because he knew one way to work off a sugar crash is exercise! He needed these guys to work up a sweat. He also needed them to replace the sugar in their bodies with something much better.

"Here!" he yelled, fishing about in the bags next to him for some old bits of fruit or veg. "Have a plum!"

Elliot took a deep breath and wound his arm around, getting ready to throw.

Because it was now or never.

He had to throw like he'd never thrown before!

BOOM!

He chucked the plum straight into the open mouth of Mr Slackjaw, who instinctively began to chew.

Yes, Elliot!

"Here's a papaya!" he shouted, his confidence rising as he launched one straight at the postmaster's face. It slid down her forehead and onto her nose, and her giant tongue popped from her mouth so she could lick at it.

"Mum – here's some cabbage! Dad – an onion! Mr Longblather – try this old carrot!"

Round and round the town clock the truck drove, followed by this epic army of sugar-crashed zombies, all still slowly stomping and moaning. . .

But also sweating and chewing and chomping. . .

Elliot's idea was starting to have an effect.

The natural fibre of the fruit and vegetables was starting to counteract the effects of the sugar. It was like some kind of antidote. Vitamins suddenly charging through bodies, powering the parts that had become weakened! And all this walking in circles was using up the sugary glucose in people's bloodstreams!

Elliot's plan was working! The town was being *de-Poffed!*

"Why am I so TIRED!?" cried Frau Fussbundler, but this was good – because at least she now had the energy to speak! She was no longer empty-eyed or drooling or fantasizing about spoonfuls of sugar. "Oh, I've got a *headache!*"

"Who threw a CABBAGE in my mouth?" shouted Elliot's mum, spitting bits of it onto Elliot's dad. "And why is Elliot driving a slow-moving truck?"

"I thought it was *tofu night!*" sputtered Dad, utterly outraged.

Elliot was delighted that people were returning to normal. But almost immediately distracted.

Because as more people started to groggily wake from their zombie states, he could hear a distant thunder.

One that got louder.

And LOUDER.

Elliot looked up through the windscreen of the truck as the very sky seemed to bend and shift above Starkley. The sugar cloud began to dissolve, and behind it, a whole galaxy appeared to twirl and curl, like ink blue ice cream swirling into a cone. . .

Sucrose Yet
So Far!

"Ahaha-haaaaa!" laughed Pester the salesman, as Elliot opened the door to the back of the truck and clambered inside. "They're watching you! They're watching us all! What a very *un*merry Christmas you're about to have!"

Elliot stared at the man. As soon as he'd seen something weird going on up above, he knew there was information to be had.

The salesman cowered at the back of his truck, as Elliot, Captain Briggs and a newly-revived **PDF** towered over him.

"Tell us what you know!" said Elliot, pointing angrily.

"Never!" said Pester. Whatever these children might do to him could never possibly compare with the anger of the Superiors.

"Don't test us!" said Hamish.

"Yeah!" said Alice. "Don't make us get Jimmy. He's got his

poetry book. We could make him read the whole thing to you!"

Pester shrugged, having no idea who Jimmy was or that this constituted the very greatest threat in Starkley.

"It's too late for you," he said. "And too late for **Belasko**. Your adults are still zonked from the sugar – look!"

It was true. They could speak again, and move around, but they just weren't as used to the after-effects of sugar as the kids. Hamish's mum and dad were rubbing their eyes and looking exhausted on a bench. The salesman laughed again.

"I could tell you what the Superiors have planned. But I will never talk. Never!"

It was no good! What could they do? All was lost!

"Maybe there's something that'll make spill the beans," said Elliot, pulling out one of the two leftover **Sugar Poffs** from his pocket.

"Where did you get that?" said the salesman, his jaw dropping.

"You forgot about your free samples! Maybe this will refresh your memory!"

Elliot jammed the **Sugar Poff** in the salesman's gob and the **PDF** all placed their sweaty palms over it!

At first, Pester tried to resist. . .

He shook his head. He broke into a sweat. He mumbled muffled, terrible words.

His eyes bulged. His ears rang. He shook his head some more.

But just you remember that core of purest sugar, covered in sugar, dipped in sugar, and laminated with sugar.

Remember that sugar baste in that sugar paste!

And that simple matter of some sugared batter!

And the blend, boil and broil in heavily-sugared oil!

There was no fighting this!

POFF!

The kids all stepped back as sugar dust puffed from the salesman's ears. . .

A giddy, goofy grin took his face hostage. His eyes rolled around in different, delighted directions.

"OooooOOOOooooOOOOooooooh!" he said dreamily.

"Tell us what you know!" said Elliot.

"But, Elliot," said Buster. "He has us exactly where he wants us! Even if he's loopy on sugar, why would he help?"

"Yeah!" said Venk. "And I could've had that Sugar Poff!"

"Don't you see?" replied Elliot. "I'm playing his own trick back on him!"

And Elliot reached into his pocket and brought out the last remaining **Sugar Poff** on Earth! There was one more left in that original box of three!

"Ooh! Gimme! Gimme!" said Pester, his fingers wiggling excitedly. This guy was full of energy now. It was all he could do to not bounce off the walls of the truck. And he wanted that next **Sugar Poff** to keep the rush going!

"Tell us how to get rid of the Superiors," said Elliot. "And the last-ever **Sugar Poff** is yours."

"Yes! Yes!" he said. "Fine! Just give me that deliciousness!"

"How do we stop the invasion?" said Elliot, holding it just out of the Frenchman's reach.

"I'm supposed to send an SOS signal!" he said.

"Nice try!" said Hamish. "If you send an SOS signal, they'll come and rescue you!"

"No!" said the salesman. "SOS means *Sweet or Savoury*! I'm supposed to pour a huge pile of sugar into the town square in the morning so that all you zombified nitwits clamber towards it like ants to a sugar cube."

"They're not zombified any more!"

"Oh, please," said the salesman. "They've eaten, like, one carrot. Do you think they are healed? They would rush back to sugar in a heartbeat! And once the Superiors look down and see that the Poffs have worked and that Starkley is under a complete sugar spell, they'll swoop down, take the sugar away, put Belasko out of business, steal your hidden technologies and enslave you all! All while you're too zombified by the sugar crash to do anything about it!"

"Happy Christmas!" joked Venk.

Elliot felt frustrated. Pester was right. Throwing plums at his teacher had just been a temporary fix. He needed to up his game.

"Then we should all get ready for a very savoury Christmas," said Elliot, suddenly feeling like that action hero once more. "Fetch!"

And to the despair of Pester, young Elliot[2] turned and threw that last remaining Sugar Poff with all his might.

It **WHOOSHED** through the air.

It BOUNCED and WHIZZED.

It knocked a hat off a policeman and began to roll down a hill towards the coast.

As Pester shouted, "Noooo!" and bounded after it like a desperate dog chasing a car, the **PDF** patted Elliot on the back.

"I had no idea you could throw that hard," said Alice, amazed.

Elliot smiled.

Elliot² Presents . . .

Come to the town square for Starkley's brand new SAVOURY Christmas! No sweets! No treats! Nothing you'll like at all!

Cauliflower Cubes!
Carrots Dipped in Marmite!
A Big Boiled Potato!
Crackers Coated in Cracked Crackers!
Your Choice of Tofu Shape — Square or Rectangle!
A Big Swede - named Bjørn!

"Just wait "til you see me cook."

Well, friendly reader, you can imagine what happened next.

The Superiors were furious that when they looked down they did not see a mountain of sugar with a river of human ants on it – but instead what looked to be some kind of jolly vegan dinner party in which everybody was reading out awful Christmas cracker jokes and wearing tiny paper hats. The Superiors didn't see slathering zombies at all. Just the people of Starkley sitting at an unfeasibly long table arranged in a circle around the newly-fixed Christmas tree.

Scuppered again in their plans to take over the world, they turned that satellite straight around and blasted off to bother some other species in the part of the universe they were supposed to be in. And just like that – the night sky returned to normal.

Elliot's savoury Christmas was a great success. So much so that everyone agreed never to do it again, under any circumstances whatsoever.

"It was so special," the mayor had said, while trying to swallow a nut-encrusted turnip, "that to ever repeat it would be to ruin its memory."

Everyone decided that they would reluctantly go back to trifles and chocolate bars and Christmas puddings for their *actual* Christmas dinners. But in moderation. And they would certainly never touch a Sugar Poff again.

Talking of Sugar Poffs, poor Pester the salesman had chased and chased that last Sugar Poff as it rolled down towards the sea. He had leapt for it as it bounced into the waters, and thrashed about in the waves until he finally found it, in the belly of a fish that had gone mad. The energy he gained from it made Pester truly believe he could swim all the way back to France, so he could finally re-unite with his darling canal boat, *Elisa*.

He was last spotted eight thousand kilometres away, just off the coast of Liberia.

And Elliot? Well, Elliot had a great time. He'd become a hero. Learned to throw. Saved and fed a town that was now singing the Starkley song while they held hands in celebration. This was a kid who went home happy. He even got a few genuine compliments on his mastery of tofu. And he still had Christmas to look forward to!

And a little later, after all the excitement of the vegan feast, Elliot went back to his **War Room** (after realizing he still had that French project to finish!) and there was a surprise waiting for him. Something that in all the excitement he'd totally forgotten.

A **Sugar Poff.** Still there, under his microscope.

Hmm, he thought, remembering he was the only one who had missed out on that glistening wonder.

I mean, one wouldn't hurt, would it?

Just one? As a Christmas treat? For an absolute hero?

POFF!

That night, on a sugar rush, Elliot began twenty-seven

brand new in-depth (unrequested) school projects.

And two weeks later, exhausted, Ernest Longblather resigned.

Pester Grool's
Make Your Own Sugar Poffs!

You will need:

A bowl

1.2 tonnes of sugar

Instructions:

1. *Pick up your bowl and throw it away because you will in fact need a vat.*

2. *Do you have a vat? You'll need a vat!*

3. *Perhaps two days have gone by and you have located a vat – well done!*

4. *Pour all 1.2 tonnes of sugar into your vat.*

5. *Add 16,000 gallons of boiling water.*

6. *Using a JCB digger or similar, stir the sugar for fourteen days and nights.*

7. Transport your vat via rail to a ferry port under your control.

8. Ferry to a remote island populated by suppressed monsters, loyal to an alien leadership whose trust you have spent considerable years earning.

9. Have that monster army do the rest, and before you know it – you've got a tasty treat to enjoy alone, with a vicar, or when brainwashing small towns!

Official Belasko Christmas Cracker Joke

Q. What kind of Christmas spy did we send to Santa's Grotto?

A. A mince spy!

GRENVILLE BILE'S HISTORY OF CHRISTMAS WRESTLING
BY GRENVILLE BILE
A School Project

I HAVE INVENTED Christmas wrestling. I calls it CHRESTLING. Basically what happens is it's Christmas and we wrestles. I'll be EL GAMBA, known as THE PRAWN, he's basically Mexico's bestest wrestler, or "bestler". At Christmas I would do my famous moves like the MISSILE-TOE ⊠ where basically my big toe detaches from my tough bod and fires off, right up into the nasal cavity of my enemy (my enemies are everywhere). I also got my moves the "QUEEN'S SPEECH", the "MID-AFTERNOON NAP" and the "YULETIDE LOG". So be aware and don't ever fight me, because like El Gamba, I'll prawn you up. Merry Chri22ers. GB out.

SEASONS

Elliot's Christmas Cracker Joke

Q. *Did you hear that oxygen bought a Christmas present for potassium?*

A. It went OK!

(Because O is the atomic symbol for oxygen and K stands for potassium and so together those two letters from the North American colloquialism "OK" or "okay" meaning "good" or "fine", so although neither oxygen nor potassium would in any real sense be able to buy or "purchase" a gift for the other — indeed it beggars belief! - when featured in this way the situation becomes absurdist, hence it is very funny.)

Hamish's Christmas Cracker Joke

Q. *What do you call a teacher dipped in stink?*

A. Ernest PONGblather!

TO: STARKLEY COMPLAINTS DEPARTMENT
FROM: STARKLEY COMPLAINTS DEPARTMENT
RE: OFFICE "SECRET SANTA' MYSTERY GIFT EXCHANGE

Dear Complaints Staff:

A lot of you have complained that the complaints department hasn't announced whether it will be doing its annual Secret Santa, where members of staff give each other gifts anonymously.

However, last year there were so many complaints from our complaints staff that some rules have had to be set in order to stop all complaints from complaints staff, in case there are complaints.

This year each gift must be between seven and nine centimetres in size so that Sandra can fit hers in her bag. It's no good giving that woman a nine-foot didgeridoo again.

Each gift must either be yellow or green, because Mr Bibbler is allergic to red or blue things and comes up in

---

Official Terrible Christmas Cracker Joke

Q. WHAT DID THE TERRIBLE SAY TO THE HUMAN YUKLING?

A. NICE GNAWING YOU!

a rash every time he sees a fire engine with its lights on.

Each Christmas gift must neither be too quiet nor too loud, nor wet to the touch, nor edible, nor inedible, nor too heavy (because of Michael's wrist) nor imaginary, NOR A FISH.

No hats (although Janice loved her tartan one from Urban Turbans) and PLEASE – remember that a two-hour cuddle is NOT A GIFT.

And most of all – NO COMPLAINING!

Yours,

Sally Rizzle, BA (Baracus), MA (Ma-mia).

Madame Cous Cous's Christmas Cracker Joke

Q. *Did you hear about the whole class of kids who went into the sweet shop?*

A. *THERE SHOULD NEVER BE MORE THAN ONE-AND-A-QUARTER SCHOOLCHILDREN IN ANY ONE SWEET SHOP AT ANY ONE TIME! ANYTHING MORE BECOMES MADNESS!*

ALICE AND THE
CHRISTMAS TRUCE

1

Away and All Mangy!

Christmas Eve is a funny old night.

It's exciting, yes, and full of anticipation, sure. But it's a very *quiet* sort of a night, isn't it? Everyone sitting around indoors, on their best behaviour, hoping nothing they say or do at the last minute might risk the number of presents they'll get next morning.

And tonight, seeing as it was indeed Christmas Eve, Starkley was just as quiet as you might expect.

In the middle of town, snowflakes flipped and fluttered to the ground, lighting up briefly as they blew past frosty streetlamps.

And down below, on this otherwise abandoned high street, was . . . well, what would you call them?

I mean, I know what they're called individually. I'm just not sure I know what you'd call a group of them. I'm not sure anyone is.

Because you get a *herd* of cows, don't you?

And a *pack* of dogs. And a *school* of fish.

An *army* of ants, and a *swarm* of bees.

It's a *flock* of birds and a *gaggle* of geese and a . . . I don't know . . . *burp* of children.

There's a *shoosh* of librarians. A *frown* of teachers. An *embarrassment* of parents.

But what do you call a big, bad band of large . . . leathery . . . slathery . . .

TERRIBLES?

No word seems to quite fit.

I used to think it was a *bruise* of Terribles. But maybe it should be a *scare* of them?

Or a *vomit*?

Maybe that's it.

So, anyway, it was Christmas Eve, and outside **The Time is Meow** pet shop on Starkley High Street stood a *vomit* of Terribles, drooling and bug-eyed and very, very hungry.

Oh, Terribles love small animals almost as much as they love scaring Yuklings like you. They love guinea pigs. Hamsters. Mice. Bunnies. Small birds. Big birds. Medium-sized birds called André. If you can see it, stroke it or sit on it, you can bet they can eat it.

But right now was not the time for this frothing, salivating *turd* of Terribles to gorge on a Christmas dinner of tiny creatures. Tonight, this *graze* of beasts was just passing through Starkley. They weren't supposed to be seen or heard. There would be no time for raiding the pet shop for snacks, no sir. They had to get straight to Frinkley, where they were supposed to melt the ice rink while everyone was indoors for Christmas. This was a basic **HAM** – or "Human Annoyance Mission' – usually given to junior *sweats* of Terribles.

It was a pity, thought the youngest of this *retch*, B'ni (and for those of you not currently fluent in **Terrible**, you pronounce this Benny). This was his first-ever mission, and B'ni was very hungry. But there was no use talking to the other **Terribles** about it, because none of the other Terribles ever seemed to want to talk. They were **GRUNTERS**, **grouchers**, *snufflers*, **dribblers** and not big on chitty-chat at all. They didn't seem to think the same way B'ni did either and were always poking and flicking him on the ears for that. Often the others would leave him out of their games, like Skullball or Volleyskull too. It was like they could sense his secret. . .

Because B'ni was a Terrible who was *trying* to be terrible. Yet it was like the more he tried, the harder it was for him. He was the only Terrible who always turned up for Terrible Class, where an elderly Terrible would teach him unusual facts about yoomans, or which ones to avoid and why, or ancient and modern-day scare tactics. Of course, he knew that all yoomans and yuklings were dreadful, awful, evil creatures. You only had to look at their weird hair and flat skin to see that. Oh, yes, he'd been taught all about yooman beings, which is why he was so scared of them, right down to the littlest ones.

But secretly, he also saw some of the beauty in their world.

Like moss.

Or toadstools.

Or mushroom risotto.

Or fat, glistening slugs.

Or a really good Pot Noodle.

Or a big long bright red rash.

And as he walked through Starkley, B'ni was even more impressed. I mean, just look at the place at this time of year. B'ni wasn't sure why, but there were twinkling lights everywhere. He was transfixed by them. He stared at them as they blinked and flashed and changed colour, and he couldn't help but gaze in wonder at the sheer peacefulness of a street like this, and. . .

Hey. Wait.

Why *was* everything so peaceful?

What happened to all the slathering? And drooling? And grunting?

B'in started to panic as he looked around.

Where were the others? Had they gone without him?

Where was his *fart of Terribles?*

The terrible, terrible truth of it began to dawn on the terrible Terrible.

B'ni was lost, hungry and alone on *enemy territory.*

Fright Christmas

B'ni knew one thing for certain: he had to get out of here.

He might have been different to the others, but being in a *wart* of Terribles was the only time he truly felt brave.

But now he was alone. . .

At night. . .

When there could be yoomans or yuklings anywhere . . . No, thank you!

He broke into a panicked run, sniffing at the ground to see if he could pick up the scent of his pack. Which way was Frinkley? He thundered down the high street, his spikes clipping the buildings as he tried to avoid the glare of the streetlights. He knew he mustn't be seen. How often had he heard stories about the horrible yuklings of Starkley in his Terrible Class? How the yuklings would try and catch Terribles and weren't to be trusted even for a second . . . How you could smell them coming because of the awful stench of soaps and shampoos and shower gels . . . How their elders made them eat vegetables! VEGETABLES! Have you ever heard anything more disgusting in your life?!

B'ni dove behind some bins as an ice-cream van rounded the corner, and hid as it drove past. What was that awful, joyful tinkling sound it was making? Why had someone tried to decorate it to look like an old sleigh? Why did it have antlers? Yoomans were indeed a dreadfully strange breed. But, oh, the smell of these bins was delicious! B'ni wanted to pick one up and tip its contents into his mouth to get to the really good stuff at the bottom. Maybe an old sock or some mouldy coffee grind or a filthy old omelette! But there was no time to drink bin juice. Not when his very survival was at stake.

He peered out from his hiding place. It looked like the coast was clear.

The young Terrible bounded up the street past decorated doorways and windows until he came to some high wire fences in front of a tall building. He knew what this place was. Some kind of yuklings centre. He'd heard of these too.

a bus loa...

carried on. He turned a co...

and quiet street.

It was Viola Road.

Of course, B'ni didn't know that. He couldn't read the strange scrawl the yoomans used as code to mark their dwellings. What kind of strange system was that? All a Terrible needed to do to mark its home was pee in it.

But what B'ni did know was that this didn't feel like the right way at all. He needed to find a forest, and follow the damp as it grew greater from tree to tree until he was down by the coast and could hear the crash of the sea. Terribles feared water, but surely his pack would meet him there when they'd completed their mission? They wouldn't call for the boat without him. He crawled into a garden to collect his thoughts.

Yes, the coast. That was where he had to be. It was less risky than trying to find Frinkley on his own. He could hide down by the rocks, avoiding the spray of the sea, and get out of this dreadful place before the world lit up again, and—

BRUUUMMMMBLLLLLED.

It sounded like someone had put marbles in a washing machine. His mouth immediately began to water. It was like someone turning a bucket upside down.

Sniff. Sniff. Sniff. What *was* that?

B'ni crept further into the garden, keeping low and breathing heavily. The smell was coming from somewhere around here. He reached the wall of a dwell-house where the smell was stronger still and, keeping his back flat against the wall, he crept round the side, following his nose.

As he reached a window, he found the courage to slowly peek through. . .

There. Look! Under the glow of some kind of weird indoor tree covered in colourful twinkling lights, there was a cage with a bow on top.

And inside the cage, a small, cute, blinking, tantalising, tempting, *delicious* little bunny. Wearing some kind of tiny Christmas sweater.

It was so sweet and so furry and so *there*.

It kept scuffling about and nibbling at an empty water pipe. It was obviously very thirsty but with nothing to drink. *No no, little bunny*, thought B'ni. *Don't try and drink disgusting water. Bunnies are so much better dry.*

B'ni was torn. He knew he had to get out of here. But there was a bunny rabbit, right there for the taking, and Terribles have terrible instincts. One sharp claw began to slide out of his finger. He started to carve at the side of the window pane, loosening it until he felt sure he could slide it up.

And then, very carefully, he did just that.

He hoisted himself onto the windowsill and squeezed through the window, knocking a small marble onto the carpet below then staring up at the bunny, licking his lips. . .

The bunny stared up at him, wide-eyed, then nibbled at its empty water pipe again.

B'ni stepped closer still.

Little did he know, but the Terrible had just made one Terrible mistake.

3

Prey, for Me!

B'ni very carefully closed the door of the rabbit cage again.

He was finished here. He should get out now. Make his way down to the coast. But his heart leapt as he heard a dulled noise from somewhere else inside the dwelling.

A *thump*.

Yoomans. Upstairs. Where it was *dark*!

B'ni was immediately terrified. He slapped his hands across his mouth and stopped breathing.

He waited.

Nothing . . . then. . .

Once more: *thump!*

Now – as is perfectly natural for such perfectly awful beasts – B'ni's animal instincts kicked in. His scales tingled and his skin tightened like leather. His eyes narrowed. His nostrils flared. He grew in size, ready for a fight. Just a second ago, all B'ni had wanted was to get out of there, but the longer he stood the more he knew that's not what his pack would have done. How they would mock him if they knew he was here – in a yooman's dwelling and too scared of a yooman to do something! His forehead began to slicken and prickle with sweat-slime.

Okay. He *had* to investigate. It was his duty as a Terrible. Somewhere in this place, something or someone had moved. And he was going to find out who. And then? Then he was sure he was going to do to that yooman whatever it was Terribles are supposed to do to them!

Slowly, B'ni stepped over the strange colourful boxes and packages at the bottom of the indoor tree and crept out of the living room. He noticed someone had hung up a couple of giant socks on the fireplace. They must have been doing their washing. B'ni gulped. Whoever those socks belonged to must be absolutely massive! Maybe the biggest yooman of all time! These were like WorldStopper socks!

Nervously, he pushed on, and found himself at a set of stairs. He was confused by the spongy material on the stairs. Why did yoomans have that? In a Terrible dwelling you simply stuck out your tongue and licked the rocks as you slid down.

The house was all quiet now. He placed one heavy foot on the bottom stair.

CREAK.

He needed to be careful. So he *veeeeery* slowly made his way upstairs. His thick hand gripped the bannister as he got closer to the top and saw a door.

It had more yooman scrawl on it. He dragged a finger silently across the strange shapes, marvelling at them. He wondered if this was a name. He hoped it wasn't a warning.

ALWAYS BE PREPARED

From the stickers and pictures, this appeared to be a yukling's room. B'ni felt uneasy. He had learned in Terrible Class that the best thing to do to a yukling was to scare them straight away. You had to really let rip. Because if you could put that fear into them when yoomans were young, they'd never have the bravery inside them to fight you when they were older.

B'ni pushed open the door with one long nail, squeezed himself through the gap and then closed the door softly behind him.

There, in the bed, slept a girl yukling. B'ni could make out the shape of her, and a mop of black hair. Okay, this wasn't so scary . . . All he had to do now was creep up on her, until he was just centimetres away from her earlobe, and then yell:

AAAAAAAAAAAAAAAAAARGH!

Or maybe **OOOOOORRRRRRGGGGHHH!**

The girl yuckling would wake up and scream and see a Terrible and scream again and maybe he could shout **OOOOORRRRRGGGGHHH!** again and she'd scream and it'd be *fantastic*. Then he could tell his pack that he was a proper Terrible now! And then they'd *have* to respect him!

So he took a step closer. And another. And, when he was so close to the yukling he could smell the disgusting clean sheets, he leaned down, ready to let rip. . .

But there was something wrong.

HUH?

Now that he was closer, whatever was on the bed didn't look like a yukling. Or smell like a yukling.

WAIT!

This was a pile of old yukling clothes arranged to *seem* like a yukling! And the mop of hair was just a wig on a mop!

BLAM!

B'ni span around as the door flung open and the lights of the room came on. Standing at the door was a yukling girl with two hands gripped tightly around a baseball bat, her face fierce and her eyes steely. She was wearing army boots and pyjamas.

And B'ni saw something on the wall that was even more frightening.

Shapes!

Shapes he had been warned about!

PDF!

That terrifying yukling paramilitary force that he'd heard so much about!

B'ni would have screamed, if he hadn't been distracted by a net dropping from the ceiling and covering him completely.

"Merry Christmas," said the girl with a grin.

As B'ni panicked and turned and struggled to get himself free, it slowly dawned on him that he should never have messed with a girl like this.

Because this girl was Alice Shepherd.

4

Always Be
Prepared!

Alice could not believe it.

She could barely breathe.

Her motto! Her motto had worked!

"ALWAYS BE PREPARED!" read the
sign on her door, and the sign above her bed, and the sign
on her ceiling. She'd put one on the ceiling so that it would
be the first thing she read every morning when she woke
up. And it was while staring at that sign that she'd had the
genius idea of some kind of net trap.

Ever since Starkley had first been visited by the ghastly
Terribles, Alice had feared she might wake up one night to
see one of the giant beasts standing over her. It was never
the idea of coming face-to-face with a monster that worried
Alice Shepherd. It was the idea of being *surprised* by one.

Alice Shepherd did not like surprises. That was why she

179

had prepared so hard. Some kids at school thought Alice was a bit grumpy, or angry even. But Alice didn't see it that way. It wasn't an anger she had inside her; it was *focus*. Sure, she could come across as a little abrupt, but that was because she wanted to get things done. And to get things done, you had to be prepared. You had to protect yourself.

So each night she'd place a marble next to every window in the house. And she'd set up the old baby monitor her parents had stored away in the loft so that she could keep a keen eye on whatever might be happening downstairs. (It had also proved a pretty good way of seeing what Christmas presents were under her tree. Like I said, Alice Shepherd did *not* like surprises).

The very second she'd heard that very small marble land almost silently on the thick carpet downstairs her eyes had shot open. She'd slid out of bed, stuffed some clothes under her duvet, reached for a wig she'd had Clover make for just such an occasion and checked the baby monitor.

And there, in black and white, she'd seen a Terrible looming over a bunny rabbit.

A rabbit she was thrilled to see, mind you. Okay, maybe *some* surprises were good. Because all she'd wanted this Christmas was a rabbit. She knew you weren't supposed to ask for pets for Christmas, but Alice was a responsible kid, she would care for this rabbit like no rabbit had ever been cared for before. And now a Terrible was about to take it from her!

Well, not if she had anything to do with it!

So, thinking quickly, Alice had pulled on a boot and THUMPED on her bedroom floor to get the creature's attention.

Then she'd pulled on the other boot and THUMPED again before scampering across to the bathroom to hide. She knew her parents would still be fast asleep. They'd opened up their special bottle of ALPINE CHRISTMAS WINE to celebrate Christmas Eve tonight. The one that stank of pine needles, like an air freshener you get in a hot car. It always seemed to make them so sleepy. Better to act now, and explain later, Alice decided. Besides, she could handle this, couldn't she?

As she waited for the Terrible to come upstairs, Alice caught sight of herself in the bathroom mirror and jumped. She might have been the bravest kid in Starkley but she could still get spooked. The blue stripe through her hair caught the light and she pressed herself against the wall to hide in the shadows.

Alice's blue stripe was pretty cool. But it was there for a reason. If she didn't dye it blue, that strip of hair would be bright white and that would make her way too easy to spot in the dark. Her mum had the same bright white stripe and, as far as she could tell from photos she'd seen, so had her gran. It was a family trait.

Really, though, that was a far as the similarity between Alice and her mum went – just the white stripe. Her mum liked to dress in flowery dresses, for example, and listen to pop songs and laugh at some of the worst radio DJ jokes you've ever heard. She would tell Alice how lucky she was to live in Starkley, and how when she was older she could get a job in town, just like her. But Alice was someone who liked to make her own decisions.

Apparently Alice's grandma had been every bit as tough as Alice and people had sometimes thought she was angry too. Alice had never known her gran. She wished she had. It didn't seem fair that pretty much every other kid she knew had a grandma to learn from or hang out with. And from what little Alice had been told, she reckoned her and her gran would have really got on. But all she knew was a handful of stories and what she'd seen in old photographs, so maybe she was just being silly.

A lot of the photos had been glued to the pages of an old travel diary she'd found in the attic one day, before all the very strange events in Starkley had started to happen. It had surprised her to find it stuffed in an old box. People usually look after family heirlooms or souvenirs like these. It made her think it had been hidden on purpose, and wasn't supposed to be found. So she'd hidden it behind some other books on her shelf, and only ever studied it when no one else was around. Her grandma had certainly moved around the world a lot. She'd seen so many strange and glamorous places. But on the very first pages of that diary, she had written something that had stuck with Alice. She'd written:

In most of the photographs, her grandma's hair had been jet black, like hers.

But then suddenly – out of nowhere – that bright white stripe appeared.

Just pure white.

Alice always wondered how that had happened, and how it had become something that both she and her mum had got too. . .

CREAK.

The sound pulled Alice from her thoughts and she held her breath as she heard the unmistakeable leathery sound of a Terrible's skin stretching as it moved. It was coming up the stairs. Soon, it would find her room and then, hopefully, her net-release button would work and trap the beast. So, as that young Terrible had pushed open the door to her room, Alice had crept out of the darkness behind it . . .

Now or Never!

Oh no, thought B'ni, struggling to be free of the net, but only getting himself more and more tangled up. *It's BlueStripe! I've seen her!*

That's what he *thought*. But what he *said* was

"BUUUUUUH RAH GUUHL!"

"Right, then," said Alice, closing the door behind her so as to make doubly sure she wouldn't wake her parents. There was no point in that. They'd only start screaming and confuse things. Let's just say that Alice didn't really think 'monster hunting' ran in her family's blood! Her parents had had some pretty scary dealings with Terribles in the past but they'd ended up just lying around in some dank cave outside Starkley while their daughter fiercely fought the invading WorldStoppers. Plus, who needs to rely on parents when the **PDF** are just a quick call away?

"You got my Christmas rabbit and now you're going to pay

for it," spat Alice. "I'm calling you in."

She pulled a walkie-talkie down from her shelf and pressed the button.

"**PDF**, this is Control, are you there?"

B'ni flinched as he heard the sound of those three letters. The ones no Terrible wanted to hear. He had to escape!

Alice waited a few seconds, not once taking her eye off this Terrible invader.

"**PDF**, just because it's very late on Christmas Eve does *not* mean you should be off duty! So *are you there?*"

A few more seconds passed with no response.

"Timekeeper? Muscles? Brainbox?" she said, a little more desperately. "Phantom?"

Nothing, just static.

Alice sighed. "Venk? I mean, at this stage, even you would do!"

B'ni stared at the yukling girl. He didn't understand what she was saying, but she didn't seem happy. He had a bad feeling about that.

"Why is no one ever prepared?" said Alice grumpily, and then leaned down so she could look into the Terrible's eyes. "What are you doing out here all on your own?"

Because that was weird, wasn't it? A Terrible, completely

on its own in Starkley, when we all know they move in bruises and scrapes and vomits?

Alice's eyes widened as she too realized this.

He wasn't alone at all, was he?

There would be others!

What if this was a trap? A distraction? Striking at Christmas, when they knew people would have other things on their mind! Hey - what if they'd sent one Terrible to grab her while other Terribles were grabbing the rest of the **PDF?** What if right now Buster was flinging baubles at a Terrible? What if Venk was furiously whirling tinsel around his head to try and keep them at bay? Was *that* why they weren't answering?

"Right!" she said, grabbing the Terrible by the arms. "Start talking! What's your plan? What are you doing? Why are you here?"

BRUUUMMMMMBLLLLLED.

Wow! That was a loud one!

B'ni clutched his tummy, ashamed.

Alice had felt the whole room vibrate with that rumble! The pens in the mug on her desk had all rattled around and her karate certificates had fallen off the wall. A few books

on monsters and punk rock and ju-jitsu had fallen from her shelves.

Alice quickly padded to her door and peeked out. She could hear her parents gently snoring.

She looked back at the Terrible. She had to be careful with beasts like this. If that was what the mere rumble of a tummy could do, imagine what would happen if he started thrashing about!

Keeping him calm would be the best thing to do. She needed to know his plan. And he was obviously incredibly hungry.

And then Alice noticed his eyes.

They looked sad, somehow. They were sort of glistening. He didn't have any of the fury you normally saw in these things. And was that a *whimper* she heard?

No, thought Alice. *Don't feel sorry for it. It came for your rabbit and then it came for you. It's only because you're so prepared that you caught it! And Terribles don't whimper!*

But still . . . what harm could it do to give him a bit of food? It would definitely be better to keep his stomach quiet and maybe she'd even find out more if she fed him. Pull the ol' *Good Cop, Bad Cop* routine. Be nice, then be tough. Confuse him. Find some clues.

Alice checked once more that the Terrible was still properly tangled, then decided it was safe to quickly grab him a fish burger from the fridge. She still had six or seven down there, she reckoned, so it was now or never.

And as she left, B'ni decided one thing. *It's now or never.*

Everything he had learned in Terrible Class had worked.

He had STARED at the yukling with BIG ROUND eyes.

He had WHIMPERED.

He had made her feel sorry for him!

And so very slowly out came another claw.

And he snipped – *Clip! Clip! Clip!* – through the netting.

He had been smart to wait. If he'd done it straight away the girl would have used her enormous powers against him. Far better to bide his time and then flee.

All he had to do now was turn, slice the sides of the window panes, and bound out of that window. . .

But as he stood and casually shrugged the net from his shoulders, B'ni spotted something lying on the floor that stopped him in his enormous tracks.

Holiday Fear!

B'ni had seen that face before.

They had been taught all about her. Or at least B'ni had. He was the only one who ever really listened in Terrible Class. On the rare occasions that the others showed up they were too busy flinging snot around or squeezing their giant bottom-spots to pay attention. But he had learned all about some of the great adventurers, warriors and dignitaries of yooman culture. The ones that would show these young Terribles how much of a threat yoomans could really be. How they think, how they move, these brave ones, fearless ones, clever ones, tough ones.

Like Karvo, Warrior of Norway.

Or Lady Alexandra, noted bugler, whose bugle-tastic bugling could make a Terrible retch from two hundred yards.

Or Vegetable Andy, the man who'd first popularized salads (YUCK).

Or this woman in a picture of the floor of this yukling's room.

This woman he recognized from a lesson at Terrible Class. The woman with the white stripe in her hair.

"Oi!" said Alice, walking in with two fish burgers. "What the—?"

Alice quickly scanned the room. How did the Terrible get free? Why hadn't it escaped? Was she in danger? And why was it sitting cross-legged on the floor staring at a picture of her gran?

"Put that down!" she barked, grabbing the old book from B'ni. "That's mine! Well, it's my grandma's! It's her travel diary."

B'ni looked confused.

"'Grandma', you know?" said Alice, still annoyed he was playing with her stuff. "My mum's mum. The mother of my mother. My mummy-mummy."

B'ni frowned. What was this yukling saying? That she'd known the great Lydia?

But wait. Look at her. The Blue Stripe.

Very carefully, B'ni traced one finger down the white stripe on Lydia's photo. And then he reached to do the same to Alice.

She flinched. But the Terrible seemed different now. He seemed interested in her. He seemed gentler. He didn't seem quite so . . . terrible.

"Our hair," she said, nodding as the creature traced one long finger down the blue stripe. "My mum has it too, but she doesn't like it, because it reminds her of Gran. She won't talk to me about her."

B'ni didn't understand the words that Alice was saying, but he understood what sadness looked like. So he stared at her with his big eyes. He wanted her to speak. And she could tell.

"Granny Lydia disappeared before I was born," said Alice. "When Mum was a little kid. All Mum says is that Gran was always away for work. She was a travel writer. It was her job to dine at the fanciest restaurants and sleep in the cosiest beds and then tell everyone about it."

Alice turned the page of the travel diary. There were a few old newspaper clippings that had gone all yellow over time. One of them showed Lydia standing outside a big building and holding a map. She had a fixed grin and her eyes were bulging like she was having the time of her life.

This kind of thing had really upset Alice's mum. She thought it wasn't fair that Gran loved her all-expenses-paid travels more than she seemed to love her.

"And then one day," said Alice, "she didn't come back from a trip. She sent one last photo, then Mum never saw her again. That's why we live in Starkley, because my parents thought it was the kind of town where there wouldn't be the chance of adventure."

That annoyed Alice sometimes. That her mum and dad had chosen a town they thought would be as boring as possible. She didn't blame them, it made perfect sense, but they hadn't taken their future child's spirit into account when they decided they just wanted to live somewhere *normal* and *safe*.

"Well," said Alice, sitting right opposite a monster on Christmas Eve, "that backfired, didn't it?"

Because things could happen anywhere, couldn't they? I mean, they'd happened in Starkley. A lot. And just think about what happened with poor Hamish and his dad.

Even though he was her very best pal, Alice had never shared the story of her gran with Hamish, because it didn't feel like her story. It was her mum's. But secretly, the story of her gran always made her feel closer to Hamish. Like she understood him, because in a way they shared something. When Hamish's dad had gone missing, Alice had quietly thought of her own mum and what she must have gone through as a kid, realizing more and more each day that maybe Gran wasn't coming home. Sellotaping whatever articles she could find into the travel diary that Lydia had left behind.

Alice knew that every family had its happiness. But also

that lots of families have sadness in them. And something about this beast made her feel it was okay to talk about it. Maybe it was because she knew it couldn't understand her, so for the first time she could say what she really felt.

"I think there are bigger things for me than just Starkley," said Alice. "I don't want to work in a bank or an office or in Lord of the Fries. I want to keep having adventures. But sooner or later, we all grow up, don't we? So what if that means my adventures have to stop?"

The Terrible just stared at her.

Wait. Of course it did. It was a Terrible. This wasn't a therapy session. What was she *doing?* And what if this was a trick? What if the Terrible was just keeping her busy until his co-horts stormed in?

"Have I gone mad?" she said, appalled at herself and leaping to her feet. "Get out!"

But B'ni was pointing at another picture of her grandma from the book. In it, she was wearing combat shorts and cherry red army boots and standing in a jungle somewhere. And from the looks of things, the excited Terrible was trying to tell Alice something about that photo!

B'ni reached over and found Alice's book of monsters that had fallen off her shelf earlier.

"Oi!" said Alice, but she wasn't quite as annoyed now. She wanted to know what this thing was going to do next. Truthfully, she didn't really feel in danger, and she felt like she'd lost some of her authority, too. This Terrible didn't seem scared of her any more. It was like he was just trying to communicate with her.

B'ni flicked through the monster book, page after page after page, grunting, until he found the right one. He held the book up and grunted again.

"What's that?" asked Alice. "Why are you showing me that?"

B'ni tapped the photo of her gran. Then tapped the picture of the monster.

""The Fleebling'." Alice read and looked at a drawing on the page of what looked like a giant jungle worm. It had enormous teeth and no eyes.

B'ni leapt to his feet, which surprised Alice, and he began to mime.

"What is this, Christmas charades?" she said.

The Terrible kept going. He danced from one side of the room to the other, enacting what appeared to be either a great battle, or some really dreadful dancing. He picked up a baguette Alice had forgotten about and began to swing it at an invisible foe, then picked up Alice's net and whipped it around his head.

"Fight?" said Alice, trying to make sense of it all. "Monster? Net?"

This was making no sense.

Until suddenly, it *made sense*.

"Wait . . . are you saying my gran went into the jungle, *fought* a Fleebling, and *caught* it in a net?"

B'ni jumped up and down in glee. The yukling seemed to get it!

"Why would she do that? She was a travel writer! Her life was all hotels and restaurants and stuff!"

B'ni didn't know if Alice understood, but felt he was onto something. He flipped through the travel diary and found another picture of Lydia. In this one she was wearing thermals and a furry hood and standing on tennis rackets somewhere in the snow. B'ni flicked through the monster book until he got to the right page and excitedly held it up.

"A *yeti?!*" said Alice. "Wait . . . fleeblings, yetis . . . are you saying my gran was . . . no! A *monster hunter?*"

B'ni smiled.

The yukling understood.

BÜÜÜÜG!

"A monster hunter," said Alice, shaking her head. "Not a travel writer? You're saying my gran Lydia was a *monster hunter?*"

B'ni mimed a pompous face and pretended to polish a medal on his chest.

"A famous one? A good one?"

B'ni clicked his fingers and pointed at her, as if to say, "Bingo!", which was impressive, as he had absolutely no concept of Bingo.

The two of them were sitting side by side on beanbags now, eating their fish burgers and staring at pictures of monsters. They were so close together their elbows were touching. Alice had never been this close to a Terrible before. Well, not unless it was clutching her, or throwing her about, or trying to chase her through a tunnel in an alternate universe.

If she was understanding this Terrible correctly, being a "travel writer" was just a cover story. Her grandma seemed to have spent most of her time travelling the world in order to hunt some of the evillest, scariest and most-dastardly monsters that Earth had ever produced.

And Alice only had four words for that.

It. Was. So. *Cool!*

Here was a woman who had tackled the Wolf-Breathers of Mexico!

Who once stood on and rode the Chinese Megaturtle!

She'd even trapped B'ni's favourite – the Octo-Whale of Kuala Lumpur!

And all while wearing a series of very stylish, adventure-appropriate outfits.

There wasn't a country she didn't seem to have visited, nor a challenge she seemed to have turned down. Hunting monsters was her whole life, and she had dedicated herself to it completely.

What had she done with these monsters? wondered Alice. Collected them for a secret museum? Rid the world of them to save humanity? Submitted them to scientists, so we might understand them better?

Alice didn't know. But she was starting to understand why she was the way she was.

And, like, perhaps – just *perhaps* – there was a greater reason than safety that her small family had found itself in Starkley.

Because just like her gran, Alice was not someone to turn down an adventure. She too was someone who'd do the right thing, whatever the personal cost. All those times she had wondered why she felt so restless. Why she was so different from her parents.

And now she had the beginnings of an answer: she was her grandma's grandkid.

And then Alice turned the page, and saw a picture of Lydia

sitting with a toddler in front of a Christmas tree many years ago. For the first time in the photos, her grandma had a white stripe in her hair. So did the child in her arms. From the top of her head, down the back, like a skunk.

That toddler must be Mum, thought Alice.

There was her grandad too, looking fit and young. All around them were Christmas decorations that Alice recognized. Her mum still used them to this day, maybe because they reminded her of her childhood. And to the side, nearly out of sight, a bottle of Alpine Christmas Wine.

And while the look on Lydia's face was one of love and joy, there was something else missing from the picture. Something in her eyes that was different to the other photos. Lydia seemed softer. She'd lost her determination. She looked . . . lost.

"Poor Mum," said Alice. "Grandad had to raise her because Gran was always desperate to be somewhere else. And then one day off she went. Never to return. Mum is still angry about it. She says that not everything has to be an adventure. She says sooner or later everyone has to grow up. But I think it's just because she missed her mum terribly."

B'ni could see that something about Alice had changed. She'd gone from a beaming smile to a look of real sadness. Yoomans seemed to have many of the same emotions as Terribles. There was something about her that made him want to cheer her up. He knew he should be afraid of BlueStripe. But what if somehow he had her wrong? What if *all* the Terribles had yoomans wrong?

B'ni decided he would tell her the interesting special secret fact he knew about the great Lydia.

So he tapped the photo, and traced his finger down her hair again.

"The white stripe," said Alice. "What about it?"

B'ni reached for the monster book again, and flicked right the way through. He found the right page. There.

Then he turned to the travel diary and tapped a photo of Lydia with black hair.

"So she had totally black hair for ages," said Alice, "And then the stripe appeared? So what?"

B'ni turned the book around so Alice could see. And Alice nearly leapt to her feet with fear.

B'ni too made a scared face.

Because on that page was a drawing of the BIGGEST,

HORRIBLEST

MEANEST. . .

. . . *MONSTER* she'd ever seen! I mean, all credit to the artist, because whoever managed to draw that was *good*.

MOTH-WINGED

BEETLE-HORNED

SPIDER-LEGGED

BUG-EYED

INSECT-FOOTED

WORM-MOUTHED

CATERPILLAR-BODIED. . .

"What *is* that?" yelled Alice, terrified.

B'ni could tell from her reaction what she was asking. So he told her what this horrible monster was.

Well, in his language, anyway.

"Büüüg."

"Berg?" said Alice.

"Büüüg," said B'ni, tapping the picture furiously. "Büüüüüüg!"

And then he began his charades again, hopping from foot to foot, making his eyes bulge and his arms flap and baring his teeth and letting the drool spill from his mouth.

And even though she definitely didn't speak Terrible, Alice was left in no doubt that this thing was DREADFUL.

"So grandma hunted the Berg?" said Alice.

B'ni hunched down and shook his head and pointed at the white stripe on Lydia's hair. He pointed at his own head. At Alice's head. At Lydia's head.

"She never got the Berg, did she?" said Alice, working it out. "She was so frightened by it that her *hair turned white*. And the scare was so BIG that it lasted generations!"

She turned and looked at B'ni as something dawned on her and B'ni could see that Alice was understanding the most important part of the story. He'd learned in Terrible Class that this was an inspiring story. Why? Because it showed that even the greatest monster hunters in the world could be scared so silly that their hair turned white! That they would give up, and go home, and live normal lives, and never *ever* come back!

"She went back, didn't she?" said Alice, flicking through the diary and finding what she was looking for. "After the Christmas photo, the last picture of Grandma is of her in a rainforest . . . *with* the white stripe. She'd gone in search of the Berg again!"

She grabbed the monster book.

Sure enough, the fanged, webbed, awfully-clawed Berg was said to live in the Amazon rainforest.

"Grandma went back to finish what she'd started," said Alice, quietly, something powerful inside her growing. "She couldn't help it. She was stubborn and fierce and unstoppable. Maybe she *seemed* angry but really she was just focused and—"

Alice stopped, realizing that she might as well be talking about herself. But now she felt a connection to her family that she had never, ever felt before. And it was all thanks to this huge, hulking, very weird Terrible in her room.

Though he would never have told his classmates, the

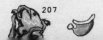

fact that the great Lydia returned to battle the Berg was precisely why B'ni liked her story so much. He had been taught that crazy woman's actions were stupid – after all, she never came back! – but B'ni thought the fact she tried at all was what made yoomans so interesting. And this yukling girl in front of him seemed to have some of the same spirit.

"I'm going to find the Berg one day," said Alice, with absolute determination. "I'm not going to have a normal or safe life. I'm going to travel to the rainforest and finish what my gran started. But I'll do it with a *blue* stripe in my hair. Not a white stripe. Because a blue stripe says I'm not afraid of *anything*."

She felt sure she would do this. It didn't matter what her mum said about having to grow up and stop adventures, because for the first time Alice could see clearly that actually, you could have a life *full* of adventure. Adventure is important. It doesn't have to be hunting monsters in a rainforest. It could be something smaller. It could be lots of smaller things. It could be camping in your garden. Exploring the woods. Climbing a hill you never thought you could climb. *Making* something. *Thinking* something. *Doing* something. And Alice never wanted to feel stuck. She wanted a life of *doing* things. Just like she did now with her friends in the PDF. Just like her gran had done!

Somewhere downstairs, a clock struck midnight.

It was Christmas.

Alice stared at the Terrible and the Terrible stared at Alice.

The granddaughter of a famed monster hunter standing face to face with a monster.

Natural enemies, somehow at peace together at Christmas.

Neither of them was quite sure what was supposed to happen next.

Merry Christmas, Terrible!

B'ni stood by the window as Alice stared up into his eyes.

Who would have thought that a Terrible could give Alice Shepherd the best Christmas present ever?

Her *history*. And maybe her future too.

And yet she still didn't know what to call the beast.

"Alice," she said slowly, placing her hand on her chest.

"Uhh-leece," repeated the monster.

Then he placed a hand on his own chest.

"B'ni," he growled.

"Benny," Alice said.

B'ni knew he didn't need her permission to leave. But it seemed . . . what's the word? Polite? Respectful?

No. Because he didn't know those words.

It seemed - in his language - RÅWLRIG.

It was time for him to get down to the coast and find his

pack. What would he tell them? Would he tell them about the yukling and the fact that, somehow, they'd got on?

No. He knew he could not tell them about this girl, the girl who must be the yooman offspring of the great Lydia. If he told them, they would come for her. She would be a prize. Oh, how the Terribles would celebrate her capture. It would make them feel invincible. They would probably give B'ni medals, and as much Blilk as he could drink, and let him choose his own missions!

Perhaps finally they would even respect him.

But B'ni realized he didn't really need that now. Instead he wanted this yukling – this Uh-leece – to be safe and happy. So he could never to tell any other Terrible this had ever happened.

B'ni looked at Alice. She didn't seem so scary now. He wondered if they'd ever meet again. Probably. But he would be in his bruise of Terribles when they did. He wouldn't be able to say hello. He knew the Terribles and their dark masters still had plans for Starkley. They would be back. So for now all he and the yukling had was this small moment in time. A Christmas truce.

Suddenly, Alice reached up and hugged him. This was the first time this had ever happened in Yooman-Terrible history. B'ni had been taught in Terrible Class that if a yooman ever touched him like this, his head would explode and his feet would fall off.

"Merry Christmas," Alice whispered, and although B'ni had no idea what that meant, he smiled a Terrible smile, checked his head and feet, then turned and leapt through the window.

Alice watched him go, darting across the street and keeping low through hedges. Bins wobbled and cats leapt from bushes as the Terrible thundered away, lost to the darkness.

Well, that was weird, she thought, shutting the window and climbing into bed, where moments later she fell into a deep and exhausted sleep, her grandma's travel diary left open on her tummy.

When Alice awoke the next morning, her mum was standing over her bed.

"Happy Christmas!" she said, picking up the travel diary and looking at it. Alice held her breath and wondered for a moment if she would be in trouble for having it. Would her mum be upset? Would she shove it straight back in the box in the attic? Instead, her mum just smiled a sad smile, then slid the diary back onto the shelf it had always been on. "Come downstairs and open your presents!" she said brightly. "I think you're going to be pretty surprised!"

Alice smiled – and then her heart sank as she remembered. If B'ni had been anywhere near her bunny last night, she was pretty sure they were *all* going to get a surprise. And *not* a good one.

Her mum turned to walk from the room as Alice sat up.

"Mum?" she said. "I just want to say that I love you very, very much."

Her mum smiled. She hadn't been expecting that.

"And I love you, Alice," she said. Her mum sat on the bed and hugged her. "Now get downstairs and open those presents!"

As Alice walked into the living room, her dad was wearing a Santa hat and a big grin. He'd probably already chosen all the dad jokes he was going to tell for the day from the *Bumper Book of Bad Dad Gags* he brought out at Christmas and Alice knew her mum was going to spend the whole day in fits of giggles over the rubbish jokes. But, for once, this didn't annoy her. It made her happy.

"Morning, Alice!" her dad said, before pointing. "Well, you said you wanted a bunny!"

Alice looked at the cage under the tree and braced herself.

And inside that cage was a big, fat, *totally unharmed* bunny rabbit.

Alice frowned.

Something didn't make sense. Hadn't the Terrible eaten it?!

"I'll tell you the weirdest thing," said Dad. "We totally forgot to give him water before bed. I meant to prepare him. I really did. But you know how bad I am at preparing. We had a little of that Alpine stuff and I totally forgot!"

"He seems . . . fine!" said Alice, delighted, and crashing to her knees so she could crawl closer to the bunny.

"But that's the weird thing," said Dad. "When we got up this morning, his little water thing was completely full! I mean, *I* didn't fill it up. *Mum* didn't do it. *You* were asleep. Do you think the bunny did it himself?"

"It's a Christmas miracle!" said Mum.

Alice thought she had a pretty good idea of how it had happened. It seemed that the young Terrible hadn't come into their house to feast on the bunny. Or maybe he had, but changed his mind.

Either way, what he *did* do was creep in, and very carefully make sure her bunny didn't go thirsty.

"Anyway," said Dad. "What are you going to name him?"

Alice already knew.

"Benny," she said. "I'm going to call him Benny. After my friend."

And in that moment, Christmas had officially begun.

DISGUISE YOURSELF AS SANTA

By Clover, head of Covert Operations
(Or 'Clovert' Operations LOL!)

What's the best way to keep completely hidden at Christmas? Pretend you're Santa! Make your own Santa disguise with my handy guide!

a. Use two PING PONG BALLS for eyes! Make sure you colour in the pupils otherwise that's a dead giveaway and you'll look like the world's CREEPIEST Santa.

b. Grab the stuffing out of something you can rip stuffing out of for an INSTANT BEARD! You can use your mum's favourite cushion for example.

c. Your mad uncle's old red DRESSING GOWN is a cheap alternative to expensive magic suits!

Captain Briggs's Christmas Cracker Joke

Q. As a noted reindeer, what do I hang on my antlers at Christmas?

A. Horn-aments!

d. Santa is often filthy from chimneys so make sure you JUMP UP AND DOWN IN AN OLD BIN so it looks like you've been out all night, glamorously delivering presents!

e. Santa smells of reindeer! Not got one? NO PROBLEM! Rub a dog all over your face and body.

f. If you haven't got a big sack, don't fret — just carry two plastic bags from your local supermarket. People will get the idea!

g. Santa is always full of biscuits and milk. Finish your look by pouring a pint of milk over your own head!

h. Hey presto — you're a cheap Santa, ready to mingle like Chris Cringle, or delight children at a Christmas party!

Love, Clover

'HAHAHAHAHAHA-HAHAHAHAHAHA-HAHAHAHAHA!'

Frank Cottrell Boyce

'Danny Wallace and Jamie Littler's books contain all the wit and warmth of Dahl & Blake at their best. IRRESISTIBLE.'
Phil Earle

'Like David Walliams, Wallace is a comedian turned children's author. Of the two, Wallace's writing is the funnier.'
The Sunday Times, Children's Book of the Week

'Original, quirky and super silly'
The Sun

'Vividly imagined ... bristling with one-liners, it has an easy, unforced humour and a strong sense of excitement...'
The Guardian

'POOR DANNY WALLACE!
Once kids get their hands on this quirky and hilarious book, they're gonna be bugging him to write Hamish stories 'til he's 97'
Tim Minchin

DON'T MISS THE REST OF THE SERIES!

DANNY WALLACE

HAMISH
AND THE WORLDSTOPPERS

'HA HA HA HA HA HA HA HA HA HA HA!'
- Frank Cottrell Boyce

'HILARIOUS!'
- Tim Minchin

The Terribles have arrived and they have a PLAN! To pause time and take over the world! Can Hamish stop them before it's too late?

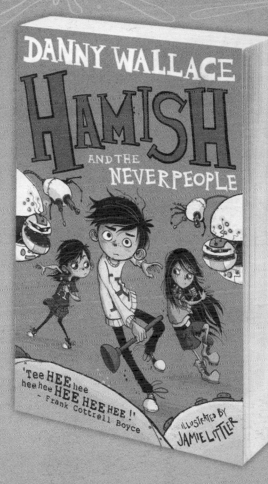

The people of Earth
are in BIG trouble again! Luckily
Hamish and his friends are here to
save the day ... aren't they??!

DANNY WALLACE

HAMISH
AND THE
GRAVITY BURP

'Chuckle giggle, SNORT!'
Frank Cottrell Boyce

ILLUSTRATED BY
JAMIE LITTLER

The whole town of Starkley is floating
on air… literally! Gravity has gone MAD
and Hamish is sure that the Terribles
and their evil master, Scarmash,
are behind the strange happenings …